FOR SALE – WITH CORPSE

FOR SALE –
WITH CORPSE

J. M. Gregson

CHIVERS
THORNDIKE

This Large Print book is published by BBC Audiobooks Ltd, Bath, England and by Thorndike Press®, Waterville, Maine, USA.

Published in 2005 in the U.K. by arrangement with the Author

Published in 2005 in the U.S. by arrangement with Juliet Burton Literary Agency

U.K. Hardcover ISBN 1–4056–3142–2 (Chivers Large Print)
U.K. Softcover ISBN 1–4056–3143–0 (Camden Large Print)
U.S. Softcover ISBN 0–7862–7020–9 (General)

The text of this Large Print edition is unabridged.
Other aspects of the book may vary from the original edition.

Set in 16 pt. New Times Roman.

Printed in Great Britain on acid-free paper.

British Library Cataloguing in Publication Data available

Library of Congress Control Number: 2004110767

CHAPTER ONE

'Bastard!' said Simon Hapgood. He moved the mouthpiece of the telephone a foot from his face, to give it the full benefit of his glare of resentment. 'Bastard! Bastard! Bastard!' He banged the phone back into its cradle.

Emily Godson looked at him with disapproval. She had a face framed for disapproval, and she used it frequently. Now the corners of her mouth turned downwards a little further than usual; her grey eyes gazed over the frames of her large tinted glasses, across the clear expanse of her desk and the more cluttered surface of Hapgood's desk, to the furious features of the man beyond.

'That's very young executive!' she said with satisfaction. 'And who is getting the benefit of your slanderous tongue this time?' She knew perfectly well, of course. Secretly, she applauded the sentiment. Had Hapgood been braver, she might even have sympathized openly, but she was aware that the line had been dead before these final expletives.

'Who do you think?' said Hapgood sourly. 'Lord High and Mighty Freeman, of course. He's made an appointment for a viewing of Milton Farm at six-thirty this evening. An appointment which I have to keep, naturally. Bastard!' The word was becoming tedious,

1

even to him.

'He who plays the piper . . .' said Emily Godson primly.

'Calls the bleeding tune. I know, I know. Freeman makes me more aware of it all the time. I'll swing for the bastard before I've done.'

'You can't, nowadays.' This was Jane Davidson, the young receptionist; she sounded disappointed at the thought. 'The most you'd get is life. You'd probably be out in about eight years with good conduct. Almost worth it to be rid of that old bugger.' She invested the last word with a proper vehemence, then resumed the painting of her nails, well aware that both actions would infuriate Miss Godson, who regarded the girl over her glasses with the disapproval of an old-fashioned schoolmarm. When the phone shrilled in front of her, Jane let it ring twice before she reached lazily towards it. When she finally spoke, her tones were full of honeyed courtesy.

'Freeman Estates. Can I help you?' Bright, professional, the way the secretarial school had taught her in their brief contact with each other. She retained the formula, and her inflections never varied. Even Emily Godson could find no fault here. 'No, Mr Freeman is not available, I'm afraid. May I ask who was dealing with the property? Ah. Well, Mr Robson is out doing a valuation at the moment. I think Mr Hapgood might be

2

available. Would you like to speak to—? No, I see. No. Well, thank you for ringing. I'll tell Mr Robson as soon as he comes in. Yes, indeed.'

She put down the phone and poked out a small pink tongue at it. 'Silly cow!' she said reflectively, and gave her complete concentration to the tiny brush and her nail varnish. Ignoring the attention of her colleagues in the quiet office, she maintained a contented silence about her exchange on the phone.

Eventually Emily Godson said with pointed asperity, 'Might the Senior Negotiator know who was calling?' The title had been conceded to her with reluctance in deference to her twenty years of service to the firm. She knew the winding lanes and varied property of this rural area better than anyone, but her employers deferred to the notion in the trade that 'Purchasers prefer to deal with a man.' And Emily, with her resolute lack of humour, her relegation of imagination to off-duty hours, her reluctance to smile in victory or defeat, seemed to do her best to reinforce this popular prejudice. Still, with marriages splitting up at a record rate even in Gloucestershire, there were many women now looking for small properties, and in these often bitter circumstances it did no harm to the firm to have a woman available to handle such transactions sympathetically. Stanley Freeman had accepted this idea, once his enthusiastic deputy George Robson had given it his support.

Jane Davidson studied her nails for one, two, three seconds, holding her hand at arm's length to estimate the effects of her labours. When Emily Godson was at school it would have been called impudence: no doubt in these progressive days such concepts had been abandoned, thought the Senior Negotiator as she seethed silently. 'Mrs Jackson from Walnut Cottage again,' said Jane when she judged she could hold the moment no longer. 'You're well out of it, Emily. I was protecting you when I offered her Simon. She wants to know why we haven't screwed an offer out of anyone for her nineteen-fifties grot yet.'

Emily winced, despite her determination to preserve a sphinxlike dignity: Walnut Cottage was a charming, chintzy arbour which she would have loved to be able to afford for herself. The receptionist registered the reaction, marking up another tiny triumph for herself in the hitchery stakes; she was becoming quite adept at this game. 'Mrs Jackson wouldn't deal with anyone except George.'

'Mr Robson,' corrected Emily, before her brain could stop her tongue.

'He said I was to call him George when the public aren't around,' said Jane with wide-eyed innocence. 'Last night it was, or the night before.' She gazed into the middle distance, as

4

if pinpointing the moment was the key problem in her day.

So they'd been in the pub again after work. Really, you'd think that at fifty-six George Robson would have more sense. Male menopause, of course. Very tiresome for the rest of the firm, though. And bad for morale all round if a painted floozy like Jane Davidson could get her own way merely by massaging an ageing male ego. If that was all she massaged. Emily bent her head over her letters and tried to banish images of such unwelcome bawdry. Fortunately, the telephone rang again at that moment and Jane was away, fluting mellifluous answers to an inquiry, taking the name and address of the caller as if they were the most important things in her life. Reluctantly, Emily admitted to herself that the infuriating Miss Davidson was very good at this aspect of her job.

Simon Hopgood had watched and enjoyed the spat between the two women. Though the senior boys had boasted of non-existent holiday conquests, they had seen little of women in action at his minor public school. Nor in the stockbroking firm and the financial services group he had failed in before he brought his talents into estate agency. In the twelve years since he had left school, he had learned a fair amount about the minds and bodies of women, but that was outside work. To see two of them with claws out was an interesting and illuminating experience, even an exciting one when he was not their target. Now he felt it was time to assert himself, with all the confidence of his two years' standing in the firm.

'Lunch for me,' he said decisively, with the briefest of nods at the electric clock above the filing cabinets. He slipped on his jacket and made for the door. 'If anyone wants me in the next hour, I shall be in the George and Dragon, sampling the dragon's cottage pie and selecting my winners.'

'You have an appointment at one forty-five, don't forget,' said Emily Godson, patting the iron-grey hair at the nape of her neck and not even deigning to look up. From her, a friendly reminder sounded like a rebuke.

Simon checked his tie and the lift of his dark-gold hair in the plate glass of the window. 'I shan't,' he said with dignity, 'though with Joe Stalin Freeman organizing my evenings I'll soon be working a fifteen-hour day!' There was no harm in a little martyrdom; nor in directing attention away from what he proposed for the later part of that evening.

Then he was through the door and moving erect and nonchalant down the High Street, his bright blue eyes studiously avoiding looking back at the office. Jane Davidson watched him pass with a calculating eye. He was becoming less of a wimp as he found his feet in the world: perhaps he might even be worthy of her renewed attention, in due course.

*　　　*　　　*

In his home, Stanley Freeman was no Joseph Stalin.

To his wife's elaborate fugue of abuse, he produced a counterpoint of sullen resentment, but there was little doubt who controlled the exchanges. Stanley marvelled at the detail of invective available to a woman not operating in her first language.

Denise Freeman's dark eyes looked across the broad expanse of Regency dining table and disliked what they saw. Indeed, she wondered what she could ever have seen in this short-legged, pot-bellied man, whose high-domed eminence had been transformed so quickly into baldness over the last few years. The too-light green trousers, the multi-coloured leisure shirt, even the gold-rimmed glasses, seemed vulgar, where once she might have found them dashing. If, as she suspected, they were chosen for another woman, then she had very low taste.

She was a good two inches taller than her husband, slim as she had been when they met in Lyon a quarter of a century earlier, elegant in simple white blouse and dark blue trousers. Where her husband's remaining fringe of hair was almost white about his temples, her raven tresses were as unflecked with grey as ever

7

they had been; even Stanley was ignorant of the small helping hand they needed now from a bottle.

'So where were you?' she said. Her assumed weariness concealed a natural sharpness; beneath the drooping lids of her eyes, Denise Freeman observed her husband closely, and with distaste.

'Last night?' He attempted an indifference he could not sustain. 'Oh, working, I expect.'

Her look of smouldering contempt warned him he would need to do better than this. He tried to hold the silence between them, but her will was so much stronger than his that he eventually had to speak.

'I had a drink.'

'Or two, or three.'

'It's not a crime.'

'No.' She studied the vase of flowers she was arranging, added an extra stem of alstromeria at the back. 'In Oldford, was this?'

Stanley Freeman, autocratic deployer of labour and intransigent head of Freeman Estates, felt like a novice mouse in the clutches of a highly experienced cat.

'In Gloucester.'

'Ah. Alone, of course?' The curl of her lips reinforced the disdain in her voice.

'With no one you know.' He was drawn on despite his better judgement.

'No. I wouldn't move in her circles.'

'You wouldn't move in *his*.' There was a

8

sudden flash of defiance as Stanley looked his wife full in the face and attempted to match her scorn. But he could not equal the cool contempt in her dark pupils, and his eyes fell to his knees as he slumped on to one of the mahogany stand-chairs by the table. He twisted the wide band of gold automatically on his thick finger; his lips set like those of a sullen child.

Denise Freeman wondered how she could ever have been so eager to marry him, even those many years before. Looking at the features puffed with drink and smoking, the stocky, overweight frame with its unattractive paunch, the seedy flashiness of her husband's clothes, she wondered how far she had moved on from the slim, bronzed French girl whose dark good looks had been so suited by bridal white. Compared with Stanley, she had worn well—but what a comparison! She must beware of the discontent she saw so often about her mouth nowadays: no woman was improved by it, however understandable its causes.

She set her face into a determined, experimental smile, estimating its effect in the mirror. She would not think about what she proposed for the evening until her husband was safely off the premises. Stanley, looking up suddenly into her face, felt laughter would bounce off those brilliant white teeth as if they were icicles. She was like a toothpaste commercial which had gone wrong. Perhaps the intrusion of such an image into his normally unimaginative mind upset his judgement, for he made the mistake of resuming their dialogue.

'He's a car dealer in Cheltenham,' he said. 'You wouldn't know him. Wouldn't want to.'

'No.' She set the flowers on top of the cocktail cabinet, moved them an inch left, studied them anew.

'It was business.' He was drawn on by her monosyllables as surely as any tickled trout. 'I'm trying to set up a deal for the pool of cars. To part-exchange the five of them in a month or two.'

'Six, with mine. If you still insist on one for your receptionist, who doesn't merit one.'

'It doesn't cost much. I like to treat her like the rest.'

It was an old argument between them. No receptionist before Jane Davidson had been afforded a company car, and she patently did not need one in the business as the others did.

Denise extracted a small dahlia she thought superfluous to her arrangement, then crushed it slowly in her small right fist. Both pairs of eyes watched the knuckles whiten as her fingers squeezed and the flower disappeared, then saw the crushed ball of red drop unrecognizable into the flower trug with the other waste. It grew a little there, raising the odd twisted petal aloft before it rolled sideways and lay still; it was like the death-throes of some small mammal. She examined the faint crimson stain the flower had left on the insides of her fingers; he had to force himself to speak.

'I can change your car if you like. I thought you were happy with the Renault.' At least he was diverting the talk from his drinking companion. 'I wouldn't get the same part-exchange on that as the Fords.'

'Better than Harry Bloxham at Granger's, was he, your new man?' It was delivered with a carefully casual air. Only the small, mirthless smile showed her triumph. They always dealt with Granger's. He had forgotten she knew Harry Bloxham.

'Maybe,' he said desperately. She did not reply. Both of them had known from the start that he was lying. Both of them knew now that his lying had been exposed. The exchange had reached its natural conclusion.

As Stanley drove his Granada quietly through the lanes, his hands trembled and he was glad of the automatic gear-box. Things couldn't go on like this. He slipped one of his wife's valium tablets into his mouth: his need was clearly greater than hers. It took time for him to re-establish his image as the autocrat of the office, even in his own mind. When he parked, he was tempted towards the hip-flask, but it was too early yet for liquor; that would come later in the day.

If Freeman had known he was observed, he might have been more circumspect. As it was, he drew himself up to his full height and checked that the back of his leisure shirt was securely in his trousers: he should be wearing tie and jacket in the office, but he had been too anxious to get out of the house to think of changing. It would be, 'Do as I say, not as I do,' for his staff again.

Four eyes watched him unblinkingly as he tidied his unsuitable clothing and took a long deep breath. Had Freeman not been preoccupied with his own problems, he would have seen his Deputy Managing Director, parked only three spaces beyond him in the small public car park. George Robson watched him curiously from the front seat of his Sierra, noting his chief's unease and speculating upon the reasons for it. Perhaps Stanley had been feeling the sharp edge of Denise's tongue again. Well, serve him right if he had, the slob. Why he should neglect his well-preserved French spouse was a constant mystery to George. Those long legs, those slim, active hips, those sun-tanned shoulders, those dark, bedroom eyes . . . Verbal speculation gave way to visual fantasies that needed no words to frame them.

A foot behind George Robson's greying

head, two soft brown eyes watched Stanley Freeman's retreating back with even greater intensity. Their gaze had been fixed unbroken upon the owner of Freeman Estates ever since he had parked the dark blue Granada. As he paused before striding away, there came from three inches behind those eyes a low, valedictory growl.

'Easy, Fred,' said George Robson, and the Labrador immediately detached his eyes from the retreating figure and licked the back of his master's neck; it was as if some spell had been abruptly broken, returning him to a life of movement and affections. George wondered if he had communicated his own dislike of his chief to the dog, for Fred was normally the most amiable of beasts.

'Some of us have work to do,' said Robson heavily: the dog would not recognize the disgruntled cliché as readily as his wife and staff. He eased the Sierra into gear and moved slowly out of the car park to meet his client. Fred sat erect as a dowager on the back seat, examining modern suburb and ancient grassland with equal interest.

And George Robson, not for the first time, mused as he drove on how pleasant life would be if Stanley Freeman were removed from it.

CHAPTER TWO

In the evening, the showers passed away eastwards and the sky cleared to a sharp blue, which deepened as the sun sank. On such a summer evening, there are few pleasanter places than England, and within England few pleasanter areas than rural Gloucestershire.

The car moved so quietly that it scarcely disturbed the peace of its surroundings. It was a Rolls-Royce, beige to most eyes, but to the man who had devised its advertising material oyster metallic. It purred through this lush green country like a large contented animal, past farmlands whence yeomen had gone to Agincourt and cricket fields where W.G. had played a century ago. The man drove carefully. He was not used to roads as winding and narrow as these. And there was no need to hurry: they had put back the appointment to nine to make sure he would not be late, but now it seemed they had ample time. He slowed almost to a halt so as to savour the silhouette of a village church against the sun's dying fire. When a man reached sixty, beauty seemed perpetually tinged with reminders of mortality. 'That churchyard could tell some tales,' he said as they glided past it. The idiom was his wife's, but the accent was North American.

14

'Each in his narrow cell forever laid,
The rude forefathers of the hamlet sleep,'

quoted the woman beside him. This time the elocution was as English as the lines. It was the delivery of her schooldays, thirty years earlier.

The woman who sat with a road atlas on her knee was fifteen years younger than the driver; at first glance the difference looked greater. Her make-up was applied carefully but sparingly. She checked it now in the vanity mirror: it minimized the effect of the few crows' feet that nowadays threatened the skin around the clear blue eyes, made the thin lips a little more generous, held at bay time's work upon the neck.

'"Rude" meaning in this case "untutored",' she said, mimicking the pedantic tones of an English mistress of those distant times. Miss Moss, she thought suddenly, recalling a name she had thought gone forever. Perhaps this region had that effect.

As if to destroy such illusions, a car appeared abruptly around the curve in front of them. It was in the middle of the road and going much too fast on the bend. It rocked crazily as the driver corrected its course, righted itself, passed them safely enough with a couple of feet to spare, and roared noisily out of their world.

'Lunatic!' said Henry T. Harben and his wife in unscripted unison. The unexpected agreement dissolved the moment of fear into laughter. He found his hand upon her arm in unconscious protection; both of them were glad to see it there.

'Probably some youngster anxious to meet his girlfriend,' said Henry. 'I'm glad we weren't any closer to that bend when he came round it.'

'It's the paraphernalia of modern living again,' said Margaret Harben. 'The swains who pursued their doxies here in times past were no doubt much less dangerous.'

'Except to the doxies,' said Henry, piloting the Rolls cautiously round the blind bend whence the car had appeared; the lane stretched empty and inviting for several hundred yards ahead of them.

'I'm not even sure it was a man,' said Margaret, wondering if this fairness was a kind of inverted feminism. 'Whoever it was was crouched very low behind the wheel. Perhaps he or she didn't want to be seen, driving like that. Ah, this could be it.' She looked from the map on her knees to the high stone gateposts which rose before them. Her husband slowed the big car to a gentle halt beside the elaborate wrought iron of the open gates.

'Lydon Hall,' he confirmed with satisfaction. He could now read the gold leaf lettering on the gates, but he had recognized the imposing

16

entrance from the brochure photograph. He eased the Rolls between the high posts of mellow Cotswold stone and stopped it on the gravel within to view the house.

It was worth the appraisal. This evening would have flattered many houses, but on Lydon Hall the golden twilight had a remarkable effect. The frontage was basically of dark red brick, but liberally laced with the honey-coloured stone characteristic of this area. In this light the building enhanced rather than impaired the landscape. The chimneys stretched towards the highest boughs of oak and beech behind the house, until from this distance they seemed to touch them.

It was an illusion of course. The trees were a good forty yards behind the house, but the long rays of the setting sun flattened perspective and made the house and its arboreal frame seem one design. Henry T. Harben did not consider himself an imaginative man, would indeed have been rather insulted by any suggestion that seemed to detract from his reputation as a hard-headed businessman. But for a moment he was moved, and not ashamed to be seen so.

'I guess I see the attraction of living here now,' he said quietly.

'You can't put a price on history,' said Margaret as the Rolls moved forward. Gravel crunched unnaturally loud beneath the great wheels in the evening stillness.

17

'That's true,' agreed Henry, glancing again at the high windows; they blazed briefly with brilliant fire as the last rays caught them with the car's movement. 'Tudor, I suppose. *We* didn't have history then.'

Margaret smiled and put her hand lightly upon his wrist. He was two hundred years out, but there would be time enough for correction when his interest firmed into ownership. She had already made up her mind that this was the property for her, unless the interior had been ruined by some insensitive modern hand or the jaws of deathwatch beetle.

'Sure is an interesting piece of real estate,' said Henry, as they eased to a halt by a studded oak door that seemed designed to hold a siege at bay. He ignored his wife's wince at the transatlantic idiom; it had been quite deliberate, a signal of his return to economic acumen after his moment of sentiment. Though his wife had her own shrewdnesses, he preferred to see her as unversed in the ways of a wicked commercial world, and he as her sturdy protector. As they sat for a moment and savoured the frontage of Lydon Hall, she looked across at him affectionately. No one else would consider her an ingenue, but if Henry wanted it that way she would go along with him. He was a good man, as well as a rich one; it was the second marriage for both of them, and she wasn't going to let it fail for the sake of small, unimportant compromises. With the unspoken understanding of the well-matched couple, they stepped out of the Rolls and stood looking at the upper windows, where a wistaria which might have begun to climb a century earlier was dropping its last blooms.

'Where is Stanley Freeman?' Henry voiced the thoughts of both of them. The only sound was the last of the evening birdsong, the only visible movement their own.

'Perhaps he's been delayed,' said Margaret. She wanted to go and look through one of the big windows, but her English reserve made it seem like spying. 'Let's walk round the outside and look at the grounds.'

Their steps rang unnaturally loud in the stillness as they skirted the high walls. There were sunken rose gardens at the back of the house, full of bloom, with the colours brilliant in the twilight. No sun crept in here now, for the house shaded this area from the last beams. There was a yew hedge beyond the roses. Between this and the trees, now revealed in their full majesty, was a perfect lawn. Though the house was empty, this had been mown and clipped at the edges, perhaps earlier that day. The wide, regular bands of green left by the mower gave the deserted place an air of the *Mary Celeste* in the silence. Whether or not because of the onset of nightfall, Margaret Harben suddenly shivered.

'Freeman is careless of his time for a man

trying to sell a place at this price,' said her husband. Even in this peaceful atmosphere, he was irked a little by bad business practice.

'If he doesn't come quickly, the last of the light will be gone before we get inside,' said his wife. She walked across the broad stone paving stones of the terrace, which ran across the entire width of the back of the house, to the big double French windows. As she peered in, careless now of decorum, the door moved silently under her gentlest of touches. She put her fingers on the handle and the door swung fully open. Involuntarily, they both looked behind them for any sign of life in the acre or so they could see. There was none. They looked interrogatively at each other, then back to the dark void beyond the gaping door. This was even more like the *Mary Celeste*.

'Should we go in and look around?' said Henry. It was a rhetorical question: neither of them could resist the invitation of the open door.

'That's what we came for,' said his wife. Her taut little smile could not disguise her sudden nervousness at these unaccountable circumstances. They went through the doors and into the old house.

The drawing-room where they found themselves was furnished with a spare elegance. Armchairs with tapestry covers flanked what looked like an Adam fireplace. There were two standard lamps, neither of them switched on, an empty magazine rack, a chaise-longue with delicately carved back and legs, a Regency side-table and bookcase. The wood panelling on the walls made the room seem even darker, so that at first they could distinguish little of this detail.

Margaret Harben crossed cautiously to the door at the far side of the room and switched on the light beside it. 'Can we afford it?' she said excitedly. She knew the answer, but wanted to hear Henry affirm it. She stopped when she saw her husband's profile, rigid with shock.

Then she looked past him, to see what he had seen. In the chair by the fireplace was a figure she could not at first comprehend. For an instant, the polythene bag on the lifeless wide-eyed head brought back absurdly the doll she had bought a month earlier for her small niece. But these eyes were no doll's eyes. They were wide with a final, desperate horror. And these lips, thrown wide against the polythene as the face fought a last brief battle for breath, were no doll's lips.

The late Stanley Freeman had not after all failed their rendevous.

CHAPTER THREE

Within twelve hours of its discovery, Stanley Freeman's death was well on the way to becoming a mere official statistic.

When Chief Superintendent Lambert arrived at his desk that morning, the death did not even take prime place among the papers which awaited him. He came upon it third down in the pile of official reports and reminders from his subordinates. The report was typed neatly and conscientiously by DI Rushton. A piece of scrap paper was attached by a paper clip to denote its unofficial status. Across it Rushton had written, 'Looks like another EXIT suicide?' The question-mark was small and at some remove from the phrase, as if it had been added in caution. The bald statement might be embarrassing to a rising detective-inspector if events proved him wrong; a question-mark transformed a prediction into a more speculative sally, in case hindsight should prove this necessary.

Lambert could not have said whether it was the question-mark which made him read the report so carefully. Probably not: he always took sudden death seriously, even in the most straightforward of situations. Suicide, it seemed, though the suggestion of the assistance of the EXIT organization would mean they would have to check if anyone else beyond the deceased was involved. A routine death, perhaps: except for family, friends and working associates who were left to pick up the pieces. But such things were the concern of the social services, not the CID.

With his experience, Lambert could piece together the scene around the body from Rushton's terse official account. 'There was a smell of drink about the corpse. I expect the PM to confirm the source as internal,' the Inspector had typed. Lambert pictured him smelling the clothing of the corpse to make sure liquor had not been poured over it after death; this clumsy ploy was a giveaway rather than a deception, but fortunately many criminals seemed still not to realize this. 'There were six tablets (valium?) in right-hand trouser pocket: perhaps the bulk of the packet had been swallowed.' No need for even the cautious Rushton to mention the PM again here. Curious though that there should be any tablets left at all if the man had overdosed; suicides who meant business usually took the lot. He read on: there was no obvious evidence of violence upon the body, no onset of rigor mortis at the time of this first, superficial examination.

The end of the report interested him more than all the rest. 'Death was apparently by asphyxiation. There was a polythene bag over the head but a cursory examination revealed no evidence that it had been held there forcibly against the wishes of the deceased. In the left-hand jacket pocket was a suicide note (no addressee or address). The circumstances indicate an EXIT suicide.'

Lambert frowned. He did not disagree with the conclusion; though Rushton had not said so, it must have been the opinion of the police surgeon on the spot. But the idea of suicide to a formula and by arrangement still disturbed him. He did not disagree on moral grounds with the EXIT organization's slogan of 'Death with Dignity'. It seemed an honest reaction to one of the age's great dilemmas, that of people living beyond the age where life was enjoyable. Indeed, Christine had warned him not to become boring on the subject in company, as he was wont to do when the spectre of his own senility swam across his horizon.

The increase of these deaths in his professional work disturbed him. The world of crime was depressing enough without the intrusion of loneliness, physical decay and black despair that were normally the province of medical men. Suicides they had always had, of course, but usually they were easily confirmed as such and the police contact with them was minimal. EXIT deaths could involve a mysterious assistant, in sympathy with the aims of the association but necessarily anonymous if he or she were to remain outside the action of the law, as it stood at present.

It was one of those difficult areas for senior policemen where there was uncertainty about the attitudes of coroners. Some took a sympathetic, perhaps a forward-looking, view; others felt that the law should be applied in full draconian severity to anyone who assisted in the death of another, whatever the motive. It meant that CID men were unsure how fiercely they should pursue such agents. Most took the view that unless and until the law was changed, they should seek out EXIT enthusiasts who translated their zeal into action, and leave the law to decide what to do with them. It was the only logical way for a force which represented the law to operate, but it ignored the fact that policemen had their own ideas, even their own sensitivities, about moral decisions, which could lead to individual anguish even as they moved successfully to defend the law.

Lambert picked up the internal phone and spoke to the WPC deep in the basement which the public never saw. 'The Freeman suicide at Lydon Hall. You have the contents of the pockets down there? Send them up, please.'

Within two minutes there was a discreet tap at his door. He was surprised to see the solid figure of Detective-Sergeant Hook, standing awkwardly with what looked like a shoe-box under his left arm and a cup and saucer in his right hand.

'Your coffee,' he offered as explanation. 'I

intercepted it on the way in.' He set the coffee carefully on the desk beside the pile of reports, and the box precisely in front of Lambert.

'After you had earlier intercepted this box, I suppose,' said Lambert with amusement. 'Oh, all right, Bert, better get yourself a coffee and join me. But I don't expect we'll find anything of great interest.'

Hook's countenance flushed with pleasure, as open and immediate as any schoolboy's. He was back so quickly with his coffee that Lambert suspected he had anticipated the invitation when he brought in the Superintendent's cup. 'Sergeants don't rate saucers,' he explained cheerfully, as he set his thick mug down carefully on the outer edge of the desk.

'Quite right, too. You'd only drink out of them,' said Lambert as he took the lid off the box. They were old companions, at ease with each other, each respecting the other's strengths.

Both now peered at the contents of the box. This moment always seemed to Lambert an intrusion, almost a violation. He took up the bunch of car and other keys extracted from Stanley Freeman's trousers, and said, ' "And all her shining keys will be took from her, and her cupboards opened, and little things a' didn't wish seen, anyone will see." ' He could never work out why it was that Hook brought out his weakness for literary references.

26

'Quotacious again,' said Hook severely. It was a favourite word of his; he maintained that if it did not exist, then it certainly should do.

'Old Mother Cuxsom and Hardy's peasant chorus,' said Lambert, instructing expansively.

'I thought that was an attempt at a Wessex accent,' said Hook. He looked into the box to see what else lay there with a countenance as inscrutable now as it had been open with excitement a few minutes earlier. Lambert was often not quite sure who was educating who in these exchanges, and Hook was delighted that it should remain so.

There were some loose money; an unused handkerchief; a wallet with credit cards, treasury notes and driving licence; pens. An unopened contraceptive packet looked by its rather dog-eared condition as if it had been carried about for some time.

'Ready for a quick bit on the side,' said Hook.

'Prepared for all eventualities,' said Lambert in dignified reproof. 'It's the approved condition since AIDS arrived. But if we deduce anything from it, Watson, it is the picture of an optimist, not a man overcome by life to the extent of ending it.'

He extracted the notepaper from the envelope at the end of the box with tweezers; he could see by the vestiges of powder that both had already been tested for fingerprints, but training had long ago translated itself into habit. He read the note, then passed it to Hook, who scrutinized the typed words:

'I can't go on any longer. My marriage seems finished. Life generally is too much for me. Forgive me, Denise. Forgive me, colleagues. It's no one's fault.'

Stanley Freeman's signature ended the note with a bold flourish. Both men were silent for a moment. They had met death hundreds of times in twenty years of CID work. It wasn't death that stilled them. It was the thought of these banalities as the final communication of a tormented soul passing into the unknown.

Hook looked at the two ballpoint pens which had been in the corpse's pockets. 'Not signed with either of these,' he said.

Lambert nodded; the signature had been made with ink and presumably a fountain pen. 'Not necessarily significant. He could have prepared his note in the office or at home.' The note was on the headed notepaper of Freeman Estates.

Presumably Denise is the wife,' said Hook. Lambert nodded: he had not known Freeman, and at this moment he was glad of it. He fastened on the fact that had been nagging at him since he first looked at Rushton's report of the death.

'He's the wrong age for an EXIT death. Early fifties.'

'What about incurable diseases?' said Hook. They both knew ill health could make age irrelevant.

Lambert shrugged. 'No mention in the note. None known of, as yet.'

Hook registered that 'as yet' with a little thrill of pleasurable anticipation. Lambert was going to take this further.

His chief was looking at Rushton's report again. 'Despite his note, there's no marital break-up that we're aware of. No financial trouble mentioned here.'

'I think the business is prosperous. There'd be something wrong if an estate agency wasn't, these days.'

Lambert caught the bitterness of raw envy; it was an unusual note from Hook, but he welcomed the evidence of humanity in his subordinates. He said, 'Any previous suicide attempts?'

Hook knew the area and its gossip better than most. He had been a village bobby for years before he became a CID man, and had never forsaken the habits and awarenesses he had found useful then. 'Not that I've heard of,' he said.

Lambert picked up the external phone and dialled a number he knew by heart. 'Burgess?'

'Dr Burgess is conducting a post-mortem examination and cannot be disturbed. Can I take a message?' Lambert recognized the stiffly formal tones of the pathologist's assistant.

'That's Mr Binns, isn't it? This is

Superintendent Lambert at CID. Just ask Dr Burgess to ring me back when he pauses for a moment in the abattoir, will you?'

He heard Binns, a humourless thirty-year-old, tutting disapprovingly. Morticians tended to be touchy about their trade. Binns put the phone down and Lambert heard his footsteps clicking away over the marble floor, towards the mutilated cadaver over which his chief bent. He pictured that worthy with apron smeared with gore and formaldehyde, hands and forearms covered in blood.

Rather to his surprise, when the phone was taken up again he heard the fruity tones of Burgess himself.

'Yes, John. What challenge have you to offer us?'

'Nothing exciting, I'm afraid. I was rather hoping you could give *me* something of interest.'

'In respect of what?'

Not whom, Lambert noticed, but what. Burgess was ruthlessly realistic about his subjects.

'Stanley Freeman. A suicide, apparently.'

'I like that "apparently",' said Burgess with relish. 'It offers possibilities. I haven't cut him up yet. What should I look for?'

'Nothing in particular. I was just ringing to see if you could confirm a routine EXIT-type departure. He had a plastic bag over his head.'

'So I have observed,' said Burgess drily, 'but

30

I haven't yet investigated the worthy Mr Freeman. You can put that down to the miracles of modern technology. We've two road-death cadavers in here that I was getting on with. Routine stuff, but then I thought the unfortunate Stanley was just that, until I got your phone call.'

'He may be,' said Lambert hastily. For some reason, he was anxious not to raise the hopes of the sensation-hungry pathologist.

'You don't let me down too often. Look, I'm just finishing the second of the road deaths. Binns can do the report. I'll move straight on to the diverting Mr Freeman, now that I'm assured of your interest. Come over if you like. It's delicious to find you playing a hunch.' Burgess knew how Americanisms irritated the Superintendent.

'You're putting him on your table now?'

'Within twenty minutes. Just the thing to give you an appetite for lunch!' Lambert fancied he caught Binns's disapproving sigh in the background.

'Right. I'll be there very shortly,' he said. As soon as he had put the phone down, he wondered why.

As he drove the four miles to the mortuary, the elements seemed to mock any suggestion of malevolent overtones to Freeman's death. High white clouds danced across a light blue sky in a warm breeze, fluttering summer dresses against female thighs as he drove past

31

the supermarket and out into the country beyond. Any death of this kind was a tragedy: on a day like this, it was difficult to imagine it was a sinister tragedy.

By the time he reached the mortuary, Freeman's body had been slid from its drawer and lifted on to the dissection table. Lambert was called through by Burgess into the room which was almost an operating theatre, with its scrubbed surfaces and channels in the floor to carry away blood. Here the object was not to retrieve life or enhance it, but to analyse the reasons for its departure. All was unemotional, analytical, unhurried: the dead can always wait.

'No gall-stones or kidney-stones,' said Burgess breezily. He set the kidneys beside the stomach and intestine he had already removed. Lambert swallowed hard. He had played this game before. Burgess would try to induce the fit of nausea he regarded as characteristic of amateurs in matters of death; Lambert would maintain an outwardly phlegmatic air through the butchery. He hoped.

'There are gowns and wellingtons in that cupboard in the corner if you want a closer look at this,' Burgess offered with relish.

'I've more respect for your laundry bill in these times of public spending cuts,' countered Lambert. He watched Burgess extract expertly the dessertspoonful or so of blood he needed

32

from the left leg. The pathologist added a drop of liquid from a bottle and handed the sample to Binns to label. 'What is it you add?' asked Lambert, drawn into the question despite himself by this measured performance.

'Citrate solution. To prevent clotting,' explained Burgess. Lambert realized suddenly that this eagerness to show off his craft came from a man who operated in lonely isolation for most of his working life. He tried not to watch as various organs were slid unceremoniously into a plastic sack, ready for reinsertion into the outer case of Stanley Freeman. The stomach and kidneys were retained for analysis.

'Nothing remarkable to report as yet, I suppose,' said the Superintendent, trying not to look at the jelly-like tremble on the kidneys as Binns took them away.

Burgess had obviously been waiting for the question. 'Oh, I wouldn't say that,' he said with studied casualness. He looked blandly at Lambert, but failed to lure him into further questions. 'Just come over here,' he said.

Lambert moved to his side. He tried not to look too closely at what had once been a man and was now unseamed from navel to chin as comprehensively as any victim of Macbeth's. But Burgess this time was not interested in internal rummaging. He lifted the arms from the body. Across the wrists, raw red marks were already beginning to turn black with the inexorable processes of decomposition.

'The man on the spot should have seen those,' said Lambert stupidly.

Burgess shook his head. 'They were under the sleeves,' he said. 'And the shirt cuffs were buttoned.' He tried but totally failed to keep the excitement out of his next phrases. 'Those wrists were either held very hard or tied at the moment of death. I'll tell you which in due course. You're looking for a murderer, Superintendent.'

CHAPTER FOUR

In the bright light of noon, Lydon Hall had not the almost unreal beauty which had entranced the Harbens on the previous evening.

In the perfect peace of an English sunset, with the chime of a distant church clock drifting through the still air, the old house had seemed caught in a time warp, with nothing visible from the gate which might not have been seen a century, even two centuries, earlier. When Lambert turned his Vauxhall between those same high stone posts, the illusion had gone.

There were, for instance, two police vehicles drawn up on the gravel forecourt. And the great oak front door, so securely closed upon the Harbens when they had come by appointment to view the house, was now wide open, so that the rectangular cave of darkness seemed to invite attention and investigation. As Lambert walked up the drive, the police radio in one of the cars blared with sudden harshness; a uniformed PC in blue shirtsleeves came hurriedly round the side of the house to answer it and explain what he was about. He argued on the radio with his sergeant at the station, who was no doubt irritated to find his staff diverted from more routine activities to join a hastily assembled scene-of-crime team. Lambert for his part was glad to see them here so promptly: it was barely half an hour since he had phoned in from the mortuary.

If the evidence of human activity had removed the ethereal charm the Harbens had seen in the Hall, it still presented an attractive enough picture. The sun had not the unwinking red glow of evening which so heightened every other colour, but it shone cheerfully enough between cotton-wool clouds. The higher sun restored a proper perspective, so that the topmost branches of beech and oak, swaying in the freshening breeze, resumed their real position well beyond the high brick chimneys.

Lydon Hall, with its carefully swept gravel drive and well-tended acres of garden, presented a scene of pleasant, privileged England. It was difficult to take seriously the idea that the head of Freeman Estates had been lured here on a perfect summer evening for the express purpose of killing him. That person or persons unknown had carried out a premeditated, cold-blooded scheme, not only to murder but to conceal the crime as suicide.

The full post-mortem report would no doubt reveal exactly where Stanley Freeman had been killed: it was possible but unlikely that the murder had been committed somewhere else and the body merely deposited here. PMs had their uses, Lambert told his slowly recovering stomach; he should even be grateful for the lively interest of the bloodthirsty Malcolm Burgess, MB, ChB.

He walked beneath the highstone arch of the front door, through the lofty panelled hall which the Harbens had never reached, into the drawing-room where their visit had been so brutally curtailed. The photographer had already finished his work; with the body removed, there was not much for him to record. The scene-of-crime sergeant was writing down the results of his usual meticulous measurings, which would take him longer than usual in a room this size. Lambert looked across to the French windows where the Harbens had entered, visualizing as best he could the scene in the twilight. The armchair with its macabre burden must have been in near-darkness: it was a good seven paces from the French window.

Two constables were covering the floor

36

meticulously with the fibre-optics scanner. In a clean dish, they had already assembled a needle, a safety-pin, a fivepenny piece, a toffee paper: probably no more than the normal detritus of a large room, but time would tell if any of these had been dropped last night, whether by victim or killer. Or of course by the Harbens: too often these things lost all significance after looking promising.

His attention quickened when he saw quantities of golden hair in a second dish. 'Almost certainly dog hairs I should think, sir, from the length and the quantity,' the constable warned him gloomily.

'Never mind, we'll have them examined. A dog here last night could be quite significant.' Both of them knew that the likelihood was that these hairs were the residue of some previous canine occupant, but the house had been regularly cleaned while it was empty.

When Lambert had been a boy eating his meals, he had always saved his favourite thing upon the plate until the last. He was aware as he now moved to the chair where the body had rested that he had saved the most interesting object in the room until last, in exactly the same way. How those imaginative psychologists who seemed to be produced at will by defence lawyers would have loved the analogy.

Bert Hook, who had arrived separately direct from the station, was looking at the back of the chair through a magnifying-glass. 'Well?' said his chief. He eschewed all references to Holmes and Watson; they would be tired levities to the scene-of-crime team, whose very business was observation and deduction.

'Some threads here.' Hook pointed to where a tiny snag in the two-hundred-year-old wood had caught a minute sliver of material; the naked eye would have noticed nothing. It was half way up the back of the chair. 'Probably from Freeman's jacket. I've no doubt he was found leaning back against the chair.' Hook knew his chief well: undue optimism would always be doused. 'There are some different ones on the leg. They might be a bit more promising.' In due course, they would be removed with elaborate care, meticulously labelled, preserved for a while like some priceless vintage brandy. All on the off-chance that they might be evidence in court, with their history subject to the destructive attentions of an acute defence counsel.

Lambert went out on to the wide flagged terrace whence the Harbens had entered. He was drawn to the sunken rose gardens, persuading himself that to explore these was not after all such an indulgence; might there not be clues to last night's events here as easily as anywhere else? The roses were planted in twelves, with each variety allotted a separate bed; it was the way the books advised you to plant to secure maximum effect, but enthusiasts like him were never able to apply it in their modest and crowded plots. They were well tended, no doubt professionally, with no sign of black spot or mildew and much lush and healthy growth. He wandered along the crazy paving between the beds until he reached the neatly clipped yew hedge which enclosed the rose garden. Then he drew himself reluctantly from the waves of scent wafting across this sunken area and went round the far side of the house, the only one the Harbens had not viewed in their peregrinations of the previous night.

There was a rather neglected Victorian conservatory here. A rampant vine dangled numerous bunches of untended adolescent grapes. There were few other plants upon the peeling white staging, and the massive pipes of the heating system looked as if they had not operated for years; no doubt the antiquated coke boiler was too expensive to use now, in terms of both fuel and labour. Beyond the conservatory, between its glass gable and the higher wall of the house itself, a car was parked. It was a dark blue Granada. It could not have been there long, for there was no covering of dust, no scattering of leaves or twigs upon the roof. It was presumably the car in which the dead man had arrived for his fatal rendezvous. So murderer and victim had arrived in separate cars, unless the killer had been cool enough to leave this lonely spot on foot.

As he watched, sergeant and constable arrived from the scene-of-crime team with their box of fingerprint powder and began a systematic examination of the car. Lest he should be thought to be checking unnecessarily on routine procedures, Lambert hastened to retrieve Bert Hook from the drawing-room from which the investigation radiated. They strolled past rose garden and yew hedge, into the arboretum which covered the last acres of the property. Here they trod on springy pine cones and dry leaves, amid the sentinels which had overlooked Lydon Hall in the days when sixteen servants and five gardeners ministered to the needs of the owners. They climbed the gentle slope to where a Canadian redwood rose higher than all around it. Lambert prepared himself to muse upon the transience of man and the pettiness of his aspirations.

'What was that?' It was Hook's sharp inquiry which startled his superior from his reverie. The Sergeant was looking towards the furthest point of the estate, where a small building could just be glimpsed through the foliage of the trees from this vantage-point.

At first, Lambert saw nothing beyond the gentle movement of foliage and the flittings of blackbird and thrush. Then he caught through the leafy screen the movement of a form too large for any woodland animal.

The shape, suggested rather than clearly revealed, was perhaps a hundred yards away, but their route to it, following the unofficial tracks marked out by the small mammals who frequented the area, was probably twice as long. By the time they arrived breathless at the point where they had seen it, their quarry was out of sight. When they ran to the straggling barbed wire fence which marked the boundary between the estate and the pasture land beside it, they glimpsed a tatterdemalion figure, moving swiftly across the rise of the hill a quarter of a mile beyond them. His trousers flapped in the breeze; the long coat he wore, even on a day like this, must have been of light material, for it streamed out behind him as he ran. He moved swiftly but unevenly, reeling slightly as he reached the crest of the hill. Once there, he turned, brandished his cloth cap for a moment in a wild Cossack defiance, and disappeared.

Hook, puffing like an overtaxed steam-engine, recognized the futility of pursuit before his chief did. They went back into the grounds of the Hall to investigate the small building they had rushed past in pursuit of this strange quarry. It was not the eighteenth-century folly Lambert had half-envisaged. It was a wooden building, no more in fact than a pleasant and elaborate summerhouse, constructed on the spot in the days when labour was cheap and the estate probably had its own carpenter. Its sturdy construction suggested it had been designed for a secure and unchanging world, and Lambert judged it no later than Edwardian. It had sides of unplaned logs and a neatly thatched roof protected by wire netting from bird damage, which had probably neither received nor needed attention since the time it was built.

For the place was dry enough inside. There was a wide seat by a dusty window at the far side, where ladies in long dresses had no doubt rested long ago in the midst of afternoon perambulations. Now the seat had upon it an old blanket with two or three ragged holes, and a faded and greasy cushion. There was also a small pile of newspapers. Lambert walked over and picked up the top one; it was scarcely a week old.

In the middle of the room was a table with a mug, a spoon and a bottle of water. Lambert picked up the small tin beyond these. The label was vaguely familiar: it took him back many years to his childhood, which was the last time he could remember seeing condensed milk. The last few slices of a brown loaf were showing the first spots of mildew in their plastic bag; there was an unopened packet of soup beneath them.

Lambert caught the glint of light on something beneath the edge of the blanket, where it overhung the side of the bench. He walked over and found three empty wine bottles. He sniffed each in turn. There was the sour smell of dead wine, but no suggestion of methylated spirits. It meant nothing: the meths drinker usually carried a flask or smaller bottle about his maltreated person. A pair of nearly new boots, too good for their surroundings, were almost hidden beneath a newspaper in the darkest corner of the room.

Sergeant Hook looked round the dusty interior of the summerhouse and said, 'Not much, but mine own.'

'Careful, Bert, you mustn't get quotacious,' said Lambert.

Hook peered through the low door, towards the place where they had glimpsed the fleeing figure, then back at the pathetic trappings of his existence. Recklessly ignoring his Superintendent's warning, he said, 'There but for the grace of God go I.'

Hook rarely referred to his upbringing as a Barnardo's boy; perhaps he thought about it now. Each wrapped in his own conjectures, the two large men walked slowly back towards the terrace at the rear of the Hall. Their route took them through a small kitchen garden, between forest trees and the yew hedge which bounded the rose garden, no doubt drastically reduced in size since its Victorian heyday.

Here a man diligently weeded the line of runner beans which climbed in impressive orange flower over the traditional row of crossed poles. Lambert coughed discreetly at the large tweed backside of the generous trousers and the figure slowly straightened. The weatherbeaten face which turned to them was that of a vigorous and active man in his sixties. He assessed them for a moment and said, with the slightest gesture of his head towards the big house behind him, 'You'll be CID.'

Lambert was not surprised to be thus identified, for most people nowadays fancied they recognized policemen out of uniform. Many large citizens in other occupations could testify to the notion and its rather random application. He was surprised at the precision of the CID label: perhaps the remnants of the Reithian ideal still encouraged television crime series to inform as well as entertain.

'Right first time,' said Bert Hook. 'And you are . . . ?'

'Bert Reynolds,' said the horticulturist, and looked at them challengingly. He was waiting for some ritual joke about his film star name: even Lambert, whose visits to the cinema had now become biennial, recognized it. Probably Hook did too, but he was at his most resolutely deadpan.

'You work here regularly?' he said.

'For the last twenty-two years,' said Reynolds. 'Full-time until last year, when I got the pension. Just mornings now. The Craigs asked me to stay on while the place is empty.

44

The lawns are mown by a contractor, but I keep up with the rest. They said to take the vegetables for myself,' he said, anxious it seemed to forestall any criticism.

'Place is a credit to you,' said Hook sincerely, surveying a row of cauliflowers with the eye of a man who knew about vegetables.

'I seen this place alive with people in my time,' Reynolds said. He leant upon his hoe, gazed back over the gardens at the rear of the house, and was plainly prepared to give himself up to reminiscence. Lambert resisted the prospect with some difficulty; he would have liked to hear about the house and its history, but time was precious in a murder investigation which had scarcely got under way yet.

'You weren't around the house last night?' he said.

'No. Only mornings.' Reynolds looked disappointed; he had hoped to trade some information for lurid details of the death he had heard about.

'Did you know Mr Freeman, of Freeman Estates?' said Hook.

Reynolds registered the past tense. So that's who was dead. 'Not really. He came here a week or two ago and measured the place up. Spent a good two hours looking round with Mr Craig.'

'Doing a valuation of the place,' said Hook.

'He didn't even look at my vegetables,' said

Reynolds resentfully, as if reminding the Recording Angel of a dark footnote in the affairs of the deceased.

'Do you know of anyone who was around the Hall last night?' asked Lambert.

Reynolds thought hard; he was reluctant to pass so fleetingly across what he sensed was the centre of the investigation. His two interrogators, trying not to lead their witness, failed lamentably, for he caught them looking back through the trees. He brightened a little as he said, 'Wino Willy might have been.' Then his spirits fell again. 'But he wouldn't kill anyone.'

'We weren't thinking he would,' said Hook hastily; already he had visions of the lame dog being hounded by a society anxious for a culprit. 'But he might have seen something.'

Reynolds shrugged. 'Shouldn't think so. He keeps himself to himself. He'd be no use if he did see anything, anyway. Mad as a hatter, he is.' He began hoeing along the line of a row of calabrese; if the temporary occupant of the summerhouse was not a murderer, he held no further interest for Bert Reynolds.

Lambert and Hook walked to the wide stone terrace at the back of the house. Then they looked back over rose garden, kitchen garden, and woods, to where the small wooden building stood at the extreme limit of the grounds. From here, it was invisible, though it could not be more than four hundred yards away. Neither man spoke; each knew what the other was thinking.

There had been violent death in this quiet place last night. In the elegant drawing-room behind them, a murderer had worked, quiet and undisturbed. Unknown to the killer, there had perhaps been a human presence, however eccentric, in those woods.

A presence that might even have witnessed murder.

CHAPTER FIVE

In the office of Freeman Estates, the staff worked quietly. Even in the world of estate agency, life goes on: relentlessly.

Sentiment would have it that the business should now be like a ship without a rudder. In fact, the office functioned with no discernible lack of efficiency following the loss of its principal. His suicide was a shock—no one had yet told his employees that his death might not have been by his own hand. They worked on, shaken a little by death and stilled to a concentration upon the mechanics of life, as drivers who have passed the scene of an accident go more carefully upon their way.

The quietest of them all was George Robson. After a little hesitation, he had moved to his late chief's leather chair and begun to sift cautiously through the drawers of the dead man's desk. He was taking Freeman's phone calls, repeating in subdued tones the formula he had now perfected, which gave the news of the death to those who needed to know. In between calls, he began the inexorable process of removing from the room the remaining presence of his late Managing Director. The small, silver-framed photograph of Stanley and Denise, taken a good fifteen years earlier and recalling a relationship long since soured, had already been placed in the cardboard box at his side, the first of the small collection of memorabilia and documents that would eventually be returned to the widow. In the privacy of this inner office, George Robson was trying on his new role, and finding it fitted.

It was a sound from the furthest extreme of the building, where Jane Davidson sat at her reception desk near the entry door from the High Street, that made him start like a guilty thing.

'Good morning, Mrs Freeman.' Jane's words rang clear and bell-like through the premises, announcing a warning to all the staff of the necessity for decorum in the presence of the proprietor's widow. And indeed, within seconds all four of those employees found themselves together in the outer office, standing in an embarrassed line before Denise Freeman, like aged retainers greeting the mistress of the manor.

Perhaps Mrs Freeman was herself conscious of the effect, for as they stumbled into embarrassed, overlapping condolences, she cut them short with, 'Please carry on. I haven't come to interfere.' Perhaps she herself was more agitated than her composed appearance suggested, for the slight French accent she rarely exhibited nowadays came through on her final word. The four stood awkwardly before her, not sure how literally to take her words, not wishing to be the first to be insensitive enough to break ranks.

Simon Hapgood recognized a moment for public school charm. He stepped forward and tried to take the widow's black-gloved hand in both of his. 'We were all devastated to hear the news, Mrs Freeman,' he said. The effect was spoiled when she did not volunteer her hand; she withdrew it with a quick, nervous gesture, so that he was left grasping fruitlessly at the air before he dropped his palms to his sides. In his ears rang the echoes of his rantings against the dead man's injustices, his gibes against 'Joe Stalin Freeman'. He wondered if the others were recalling such moments; the thought atrophied his tongue in a dry mouth.

It was Emily Godson who saved the situation. She had seen more of suffering and death than anyone there, and she reacted instinctively where the rest were awkward. 'Come through to the rest-room and I'll make some tea,' she said. It was as natural and warm as Hapgood's gesture had been stilted, and Denise Freeman allowed herself to be led away. The two women moved past the long display panels with their colour photographs of houses, past filing cabinets and computer, into the small room which served as a refuge from the public for coffee- and lunch-breaks. It was scarcely more than a small converted kitchen, but it had a microwave oven, a kettle, a sink and two small armchairs. Most precious of all, it offered privacy when business was hectic, once the door to the main office was shut.

Emily sat the widow in the more comfortable armchair and set about the deliberate ritual of making tea. She was not an acute woman, but some instinct told her that the everyday preparation of this small comfort would restore control to this very different woman as it did to her. Denise was a year or two younger than she was, but she treated her as if she were an old woman or a child, who in the trauma following death could be soothed by having small decisions made for her. And Denise Freeman, shocked and lonely at this moment of entry into her husband's former domain, allowed herself to be mothered. She scarcely ever drank tea, and then with lemon only, but now she accepted Emily's prescription of strong, hot tea with milk and sugar, and eventually sipped it without demur.

'I can't believe it!' she said conventionally. In truth she was calm enough, though she had

50

been thrown off balance for a moment by the confrontation with her late husband's colleagues, and one of them in particular.

'That's only natural. It will take time to come to terms with it,' said Emily Godson. Fortunately, clichés did not ring false in her ears, and she was even able to say with conviction, 'You mustn't blame yourself, you know.'

'I shan't,' said Denise, with a touch of her normal acerbity and the faintest of smiles. Emily went over to the kettle to replenish the teapot, and took advantage of the move to examine Stanley Freeman's widow carefully in profile.

She looked composed enough. The long black hair, tied back in the French style Emily had always found rather severe, was as neat and lustrous as ever. She was a little pale, but that was only to be expected, and she was always sallow anyway. She wore a simple black dress and gloves, but the patent leather shoes, carefully pinned white scarf and small diamond brooch showed careful attention to detail: this woman had examined herself carefully in a full-length mirror before she left home. Emily, who had grown used to comfortable shoes and cardigans, was shocked at the mannequin-sharp appearance of the widow. Grief, she thought vaguely, should be less organized than this.

Denise Freeman, though, seemed genuinely

grateful as she thanked the Senior Negotiator for her ministrations. She moved quietly back into the outer office, where she had a word with each of the other workers in turn and tried not to act like visiting royalty. She was shocked how white and drawn Jane Davidson looked at the reception desk. Perhaps it was only the wrong time of the month for her, but she seemed rather abrupt and abstracted even as she dealt with telephone inquiries, where she was normally at her best. There was little colour even in her lips; the vivid red of her nails and the blue veins of her forearms, the small red scratch on the back of her hand, stood out unnaturally, as if she were made up for a horror film.

'Nothing we can't cope with, Mrs Freeman,' she said in answer to Denise's inquiry, but the little laugh which followed rang brittle as crystal in the unusually quiet office. Denise thought of how she had grudged this girl her company car, and felt a pang of guilt, for Jane seemed more upset by Stanley's death than anyone.

Simon Hapgood had composed himself in the interval since his false start with the widow. He ventured no physical contact this time, but managed to make the necessary platitudes sound sincere enough. 'If there's anything at all we can do to help, don't hesitate to ask,' he said. He stood erect and without apparent embarrassment, but now kept his desk

52

between himself and their visitor. 'It can't be an easy time.'

Before Denise Freeman could reply, he spied a customer in the doorway and hastened to prove his indispensability to the firm. 'Ah, Mr Rostron, do come and sit down. The cottage at Windrush, wasn't it?' As Denise moved on, she heard him talking in low, confidential tones to the newcomer, no doubt explaining the unusual and tragic circumstances which beset them all this morning. As she went with George Robson into the office that had been her husband's, her last image was of the anxious white oval of Jane Davidson's face, watching her as if bewitched over Hopgood's subdued exchange with his client.

Robson had had time to regain his self-possession. 'Sorry to move into Stanley's desk so quickly,' he said, avoiding just in time a reference to dead men's shoes, 'but the demands of the business made it unavoidable. I'm having to rearrange all Stanley's calls.' He charitably refrained from telling the grieving widow that there were precious few of them. They had carried their late chief for long enough: people would soon see how the policy and drive in this place came from George Robson. He felt something very like exhilaration, already.

'I'm taking most of them myself, of course. Mrs Godson insisted on taking one file. An elderly maiden lady, she said. Well, she's better with them than I am!' He was talking too much, sidetracked for a moment by the concerns of the agency when he should have been finding a more personal note. 'Is there anything I can do for you, Denise?' He ventured the Christian name; it came out naturally enough.

Denise shook her head with a quick, abstracted smile. She looked well in black; very well, he thought. Grief, if grief there was, sat well upon her. She had kept her figure and her looks while her husband had run to seed. He found himself wondering whether beneath the demure black dress there was skimpy black underwear. Hastily banishing the thought and raising his eyes to her face, he found Denise's dark eyes looking into his. With amusement, he could have sworn; certainly not outrage, anyway. She was as tall as Robson, and their eyes were not far apart: it was his which dropped first, as he strove to concentrate upon matters more appropriate to the moment. Had she caught his instant of lust, and not been outraged? That Freeman had been a sluggish, neglectful oaf. She had been wasted on him for far too long. It wasn't surprising she had looked for consolation elsewhere, even while he was alive. Perhaps in time . . .

'Not short of money, are you?' he said. 'People in these circumstances often find they have a temporary—'

'Not short of anything, thank you, George,' said Denise. She put her hand briefly upon the back of his and smiled at him. 'Just you get into Stanley's seat and pick the business up. That's the best thing you can do for me at the moment. Any large decisions, I shall be around. All the day-to-day stuff, carry on regardless.'

Having thus asserted her pre-eminent position, Denise Freeman pulled on her black fabric gloves and prepared to depart. Robson wondered if she knew the full details of the disposal of the business contained in the will, or whether it would be a surprise to her. Time would tell: he saw himself expansive and magnanimous, his arm around the slim shoulders of a submissive Denise.

He escorted her to the door, assuming already the panache of the principal of the firm seeing an important visitor off the premises. The role, he felt, sat naturally upon him.

And the outer office duly played its supporting role. Simon Hapgood was taking the details of an offer on the cottage at Windrush; Jane Davidson was arranging a viewing on the phone; Emily Godson was appending a 'Sold, Subject to Contract' strip to one of the houses on the display panel.

It suited Denise Freeman to play the fragile widow. She allowed herself to be guided through familiar territory by the expansive

George Robson. And the curious Emily God-son, the careful Simon Hapgood and the pallid Jane Davidson observed the performance of the pair with interest.

In the coming days, each would feel the impact of last night's death. As yet, the revelation that the police were treating the case as murder had been made to none of them.

Yet one of them at least knew exactly how Stanley Freeman had died.

CHAPTER SIX

Hook got out at the entrance to the Crown Hotel. By the time Lambert had parked the big Vauxhall, his sergeant was genuflecting reverently before the gleaming beige Rolls-Royce.

'Oh, thou worshipper of Mammon,' said the Superintendent, 'will I never succeed in wooing you from the trappings of materialism?'

'I was examining the motif,' said Hook, enunciating the exotic word with relish, 'and thinking how inferior it is to the old Winged Victory.'

'A lady who exacted a savage toll in road accidents, as you should know,' said Lambert severely.

'Thus removing drunken pedestrians from this sordid world to a better place,' said Hook, with a triumphant logic that was apparent to him, if not to his chief and the drayman bystander.

Lambert looked at the HTH on the number plate and said, 'If you wish to maintain these links with affluence, I fancy we are about to interview the owner of this splendid vehicle.'

The Crown did not offer suites, but Mr and Mrs Harben had been afforded the privacy of the manager's flat to meet the detectives. They sat there a little self-consciously, having placed themselves carefully in armchairs and moved the sofa a fraction to accommodate their visitors. The big room with its flowered carpet felt rather like a stage set as they waited for Lambert and Hook to make their entrance and set the scene in motion.

This impression was heightened by the simultaneous arrival of a maid in black and white uniform, sent in by the manager with coffee and cream in an elegant silver service. Lambert exchanged meaningless opening pleasantries with the Harbens while the maid unloaded cups, saucers, spoons, coffee-pot, jug and sugar bowl in seeming slow motion, with every sound echoing in the large, low-ceilinged room; all four of the principals waited for the maid to depart so that the real dialogue could commence. Lambert found himself caught up in the effect, trying not to clear his throat

57

before his opening speech. This should be no more than routine stuff.

'We always talk to the people who discover the body in cases of sudden death. I know you spoke to Detective-Inspector Rushton briefly last night. We may need to duplicate some of that conversation. It shouldn't take long. I'm sorry if your holiday plans have been disrupted.'

'It isn't just a vacation,' Harben corrected him automatically. 'We're hoping to live in this area. That's why we were looking at Lydon Hall last night.'

Lambert nodded. 'You had an appointment to do so?'

'Yes. For nine o'clock.'

'You're sure of the time?'

'Yes. I changed it. Originally it was eight-thirty, but we had another property to look at near Hereford, and I knew we couldn't make the Hall much before nine.'

'How did you change the time of the appointment, Mr Harben?'

Harben looked at his wife. 'Margaret did it.'

Margaret Harben came in quickly. 'That's right. I used the car phone.'

'Can you recall what time that would be?' Lambert was calm and impassive, watching the faces before him as carefully as if they had been suspects; it was Hook who was noting down the detail of the replies.

'Oh, I should think about two-thirty

yesterday afternoon. It was after lunch and before we got to Worcester. Is it important?' She was just a little tetchy, resenting this level of questioning about a routine death. The whole business had upset her rather more than she cared to admit, even to herself. As one who had not come face to face with this sort of death before, she was shaken by the thought of the chasm of despair which must open up before a suicide. Yet she also resented Stanley Freeman's decision to end his days with such an unwarranted intrusion into her life. She had fallen in love with Lydon Hall, and felt it had rnade a favourable impression on her hard-headed husband. Freeman's death had spoiled that. She might never live there now, and she blamed the man she had never met for his untimely and ill-chosen death. It might be unworthy and petty in her, but that thought only increased her irritation.

'Probably not,' said Lambert, with a smile which disconcerted her even further by its suggestion that he knew all about her resentment against the dead man. 'But it could be. We shall need to check all the facts around the case, set each person's recollections against those of others, see if there are significant differences. We have to start somewhere, so we begin with you and your husband as the discoverers of the body.'

Henry T. Harben was fascinated by this initiation into British police procedure, but felt he had been silent long enough.

'I'm impressed by this attention to detail, Superintendent, but isn't it just a little over the top? I guess your English thoroughness is just great, but I can't see the New York police spending this kind of time and resources on a routine suicide.' His smile emphasized that on this occasion at least common sense was on the side of the New World.

'Oh, I think they might—once they realized that someone had been trying to dress up murder as suicide!' said Lambert with an answering smile. He tried to be sorry for structuring his revelation into a small drama, but in truth such little pleasures were small compensation for the many hours of dull fact-finding which were the normal lot of the CID. He was gratified by the widening eyes of the Harbens. Into Margaret's face there gradually seeped distress, as she struggled to come to terms with the fact that the scene still printed upon her memory from last night embodied not just the self-destruction of an unhappy man but some other, more evil presence as well. She tried the easiest option first.

'Maybe the law says it's murder. But most of us wouldn't think of someone who assisted an EXIT suicide as a murderer. More as a compassionate and courageous final friend in need, I'd say.'

Harben looked sharply sideways at his wife. Perhaps it was a side of her he had not seen before; perhaps he had merely not heard of an organization designed to facilitate this kind of death. His grey hair was dishevelled a little now, where he had run a hand through it; he looked older, as if prosperity had suddenly lost its proficiency to keep time at bay.

Lambert glanced at the inscrutable Hook, as he usually did when he was about to reveal more than he should. He said quietly, 'I'm afraid all the indications are of a different sort of killing, Mrs Harben.' He reached into his inside pocket for the single sheet of paper which would make it official in her mind, picked out and read to her the phrases he already knew by heart. 'This is the preliminary post-mortem report. "Death was by asphyxiation. It is unlikely that this could have been voluntary asphyxiation. The plastic bag which was the instrument of death appears to have been held around the neck. Abrasions on the wrists and bruising on the upper left arm are commensurate with the restraining of the arms from the rear at the time of death . . . A meal of chicken, chips and peas had been eaten some two hours before death. A quantity of whisky approximating to five single measures had been consumed in the period immediately before death."'

He looked through the rest of the notes, deliberately low-key. 'There are other details, principally about the time of death, but I think that thanks to your evidence we can already be

61

– more precise than the pathologist in this respect. The post-mortem report will all be dressed in more cautious medical language for the inquest, but the gist of it is what I've told you.'

He paused and watched a process he had seen many times before; the reality of villainy seeping into the minds of the innocent. The thoughts of Henry and Margaret Harben were back in Lydon Hall at sunset, its loveliness clouded now with the presence of evil. While they had strolled in elation around the gracious house which might have become their home, a murderer's victim had lain within and the murderer himself had been nearby, had possibly even watched their movements. Lambert, familiar with this moment, could almost follow the thought processes. It was time to resume routine.

'Do you know what time you arrived at the Hall? As exactly as possible, please.'

'It must have been just a minute or so before nine. We parked at the gates. A church clock struck as we walked round the side of the house.' This was Henry Harben, pouring out facts as if they were an assertion of innocence.

'Did either of you see anyone anywhere around the house?'

Margaret Harben gave a little shudder of repugnance before she replied, for the implication of the question was clear enough.

'No one.'

'You realize the importance of this. When you went to the rear of the house, how far into the grounds did you go?'

They looked at each other. Henry Harben's baritone drawl was strangely reassuring as he said, 'We strolled along the terrace and looked at the rose gardens.'

'You didn't go any further back, towards the woods behind?'

'No. We were waiting for Stanley Freeman to arrive. We didn't go into the arboretum.' Lambert was surprised at his use of the technical word, then realized it would have been on the particulars of the Hall put out in the agent's brochure.

'You caught no sign of any human movement as you looked at the woods?'

'No. Did the killer go that way?'

'I've no idea. We have reason to think, though, that someone may have been in the arboretum at the time of the murder.' Inwardly, Lambert cringed as he always did at the jargon of his trade, but he could not deny the usefulness of these circumlocutions at times.

'You mean that while we were finding the body, the murderer might have been watching our every move from out there?' Margaret Harben was white with the notion. Sometimes witnesses enjoyed the vicarious horror of such melodrama, from a safe retrospect; she seemed merely shaken at the thought of how

63

near evil had been to them while they walked in innocent survey.

'It's possible. It's also possible that someone as guiltless as you was around rather earlier, and saw more. If so, we'd obviously like to locate that person.'

Harben put his hand over his wife's, where it gripped the arm of the chair. 'We didn't see anyone, Superintendent.'

'Let's concentrate on the house, then. How did you enter the house?'

'The French window wasn't locked.' Margaret Harben was defensive with an English respect for private property. 'It wasn't even latched. It opened when I touched it.'

'You went straight into the drawing-room?'

'We thought Freeman must be in the house,' said Harben.

'And he was. In a manner of speaking,' said Lambert. 'Did you find him immediately?'

'As soon as I put the light on. Until then, we thought the room was empty.' Margaret Harben was tight-lipped with the memory of the moment.

'Did you go any further into the house?'

'No.'

'You're sure of that? You didn't go beyond the door of the drawing-room?'

'No. Is it important?'

Lambert ignored the question for a moment. 'Where did you phone from?'

'From the car. I have a phone in the Rolls.

We went back there,' said Harben.

'And you rang the police?'

'There was no hurry about an ambulance. I used to be a nurse, remember,' said Margaret Harben. Lambert, who could scarcely be expected to remember what he had never been told, was familiar with this assumption of omniscience among those he questioned.

'Did you go back to the Hall after you'd dialled 999?'

They looked at each other. 'No. We sat in the car at the gates until your policemen arrived. Is it important?' Harben's impatient tone implied that it was not.

'It could be. Someone could have been in the house, anywhere beyond that drawing-room door, when you discovered the body.'

'The murderer could still have been there.' Margaret Harben's face etched the sickly excitement of the thought.

'It's possible. The uniformed men searched the house when they arrived, as part of the normal routine, and found no one.'

'But we were at the gates until they came. We would have seen anyone leave.' This was Harben. He was anxious to dismiss the material for nightmares from his wife's mind, though Lambert judged that now she was enjoying the frisson of a danger that was past.

'By orthodox means, yes. But of course anyone could have left the house from the rear and disappeared through the arboretum.'

He was right: Margaret Harben was hugging to herself her involvement in what she now saw as a melodrama rather than a sad suicide. She was at this moment more determined than ever to buy Lydon Hall, suddenly impatient to be alone with her husband to sound his feelings in the matter, yet reluctant to relinquish her involvement in the inquiry. 'What else do you want to know?' she said.

'You'll have realized by now that I'm trying to assemble every known fact surrounding the death of Stanley Freeman, from yourself and others. The hope is that one or more of those facts will eventually emerge as significant. We've covered your arrival at the house, your discovery of the body, and the period between that moment and the arrival of the police. All that remains is the period immediately before that. In driving to visit the Hall, did you see or hear anything significant in the area?'

He did not need to issue the usual injunctions to take time and think carefully; these witnesses were anxious to be of help. There was quite a pause before Margaret Harben said reluctantly, 'I don't think so.'

Lambert waited, letting the dubious recall of the subconscious have its final chance. Unexpectedly, it was Henry T. Harben who spoke, his transatlantic tones suddenly sharpened with the thrill of his recall.

'We passed a car. Going far too fast. On a bend.'

'How near to the house?' Lambert was professionally matter-of-fact.

'Half a mile, perhaps.'

'Make and model?'

'I couldn't be certain of either. It came out of the sun. I was glad enough to miss it.'

'Colour?'

'Blue?' He looked at his wife, who nodded her agreement.

'Did you see the driver?'

The Harbens looked at each other, intense with concentration, then shook their heads in simultaneous frustration. Henry said, 'The windscreen was right against the sun. In any case, I was fighting to avoid a collision.'

The four people in the room looked at each other, revolving the single thought. Perhaps only the murderer's desperate speed in departure had preserved his anonymity. Or hers.

CHAPTER SEVEN

Denise Freeman rolled on to her back and stretched a slim brown arm to pick up her watch from the bedside table. 'One o'clock. Time you were going,' she said to her lover.

He stretched his feet to the end of the bed in heavy, post-coital lassitude, and tried to pretend everything was as it had always been.

'Five minutes,' he said with a satisfied smile. In truth, it had not been as satisfactory as they had expected: Simon Hapgood knew that as well as Denise.

She looked down at the small aureole of yellow hair around his head as he sank it back into the silken pillow. His eyes were closed, his face smooth-skinned and relaxed, the small, attractive smile fixed upon the quiet lips. His lovemaking had been as urgent, as fierce, as uncomplicated as ever. And she had responded as always, fitting her passion to his violence, surging to a climax without needing any refinement of technique from him. That brief moment of concerted frenzy had been as successful as ever.

Yet this time it had been only a moment. They had been as awkward before it as they had been that first time many months ago. The words which normally came so easily to her had had to be framed by deliberate thought, and that had made the speaking of them a self-conscious exercise. They had kissed briefly, peremptorily even, with none of the slow, exploratory excitement of lovers secure in their attraction. And today she had found within her mouth the sour taste of death.

On the second day after his death, Stanley Freeman had inhibited them as he never had in life. She had been conscious as she never had before of making love in Stanley's house with another man. A younger man. A lover not so very different from what Stanley had been once: she had never had that thought before. Perhaps her conscience, if her feelings could be dignified as anything so worthy, should have been more active when her husband was alive. The thought did not help her now.

'I've got to move,' she said. She rolled her legs over the side of the bed and reached for her towel robe: with a lover twelve years your junior, it was important he should not have a detailed view of sagging curves as they disappeared towards the shower. For the first time she could remember, she was not reluctant to leave him.

Simon Hapgood listened to the soothing hiss of the shower and wondered why he too felt so deflated today. He was too self-centred to allow that Stanley Freeman, a man he had both disliked and despised, could have troubled him so much more in death than in life. Of course, the fact of his death had changed the situation; that was indisputable. The lines were bound to be re-drawn, and as yet he was not sure how. Would Denise expect him now to marry her? What had been a passionate, breathtaking affair of stolen hours and uncertain future had now no barriers to prevent it becoming permanent.

Would he, indeed, want to marry Denise? He had never thought about it until now. He could certainly use all this: he looked round the bedroom, with its quality built-in furniture, its cut-glass chandelier and wall lights with their suggestion of *fin-de-siècle* sensualities, its brass-handled mahogany door to the en suite bathroom where his mistress was showering. He stretched his limbs indulgently against the silk sheets. Opulently fitted, he would call it if he were describing the house for the market: and that's what his life would be if he married Denise. He had already discarded any notion that she might not be delighted to marry him.

He tried to analyse his feelings for Denise Freeman, without much success. He was not given to self-analysis, the result being too often depressing, and he found it difficult to be objective. He felt a strong but nevertheless shallow affection for Denise; it was probably as much as he had felt for anyone in an unsatisfactory life. Was it more than sexual desire and gratification? She had been kind, understanding, experienced, and his own bedroom performance had blossomed as a result. Under her patient hand, he had almost said. He looked at the long mirrors of the wardrobe doors and smiled at his tousled hair and flushed face.

In the bathroom, Denise Freeman towelled herself vigorously, rubbing away the introspective depression that had preceded and followed their lovemaking. As she brushed the long black hair which now hung straight and free over her shoulders, Simon would not have been flattered by her thoughts. He would indeed have been disturbed. For Denise was pondering upon just when and how she should dispense with him.

It had been a satisfactory affair. When Stanley was alive, it had combined excitement, danger, and a sexual gratification she had long since ceased to find in her marriage. Simon Hapgood was rather splendidly handsome in an effete sort of way. That he was a fairly junior employee of her husband's added an extra frisson to the relationship; it also made the affair easier to conduct for one of her organizational skills, for she could be aware of the appointments and working arrangements of both parties. Stolen hours of lust (she was still not sure how much more than that was involved) were much more successful when the threat of discovery and embarrassing confrontations remained small. Under her competent supervision, the boundaries had been clear and the affair manageable. Now that the lines had been obliterated, she would have to draw new ones. That was only to be expected. What she had not taken into acocunt was this belated and wholly unexpected feeling of guilt, this soft-centred regret for her dead husband, this self-recrimination about the golden early years of her marriage and the missed opportunities of later times.

She emerged half-dressed from the bathroom, brusquely dismissing her uncertainties. 'Time you were moving, lover-boy,' she said. Perhaps she knew the strange attractiveness her slight French accent gave to the glib phrases of Hollywood. She took a dress that was scarcely worn from the wardrobe. Trousers suited her long legs and slim hips, emphasized the measurements she had retained since she was twenty-one, but policemen should be received conventionally. She would make no gesture towards mourning: curiously, her unexpectedly tender recall of her husband made her more sensitive to the effects she might create. Black might be construed as hypocritical by anyone who knew of the recent state of her marriage. She had not enjoyed her visit in black to the offices of Freeman Estates, and Simon had scarcely helped things by going over the top when he should have kept quiet. She chose a dark pink summer dress, demure, but light enough to sketch in her trim bust and waist with every movement she made.

'What time are they coming?' Simon made no attempt to move as he watched her pull the dress over her tanned shoulders. She must be ten years, maybe even a little more, older than his thirty, he thought. But she had worn well, there was no disputing that. And certainly in bed—

'In half an hour. Come on, darling. Out!' She slapped his thigh and pulled away the clothes. He rolled reluctantly out and reached for his shirt: he was still not secure enough to parade himself naked before her experienced eyes. He washed and dressed quickly; he had no wish to meet senior policemen, in however routine a context. When he emerged from the bathroom, Denise had left the bedroom.

When he was a vigorous forty-eight, she would be almost sixty, he mused. When he was fifty-eight, she would be an old lady. They said older women were grateful, the raffish, inadequate young men with whom he exchanged notes. Most of them aspired to a rakishness they would never achieve. Simon was obscurely aware of this, so he did not rate their opinions very highly. But he was not good at leaps of imagination, so that picturing this long-term future, weighing the pros and cons of marriage to a rich and sexually voracious widow, was beyond him. He did not yet know it was a pointless exercise.

'I have an appointment at two myself anyway,' he said. He vaguely resented the way she seemed always to manage the length and termination of their meetings, and was trying to assert his own measure of control. 'What does this policeman want?'

'Superintendent Lambert,' she said, unconsciously adopting the precision she found necessary. 'Is Superintendent a high rank in the British police?'

'Very,' said Hapgood. 'Too high to be wasting his time on this!'

As she turned away from him, Denise's face

twitched as if she had been slapped: the notion that Stanley's death should be unworthy of the attention of anyone significant seemed insensitive from one who had invaded his bed. She told herself she was being unfair: this very directness in Simon had once been an attraction to her.

'Do they know about us?' Simon was defensive; he had seen quite enough of policemen in the past.

'There's no way they can do.'

'It's better to keep it that way.' There was something very near alarm in his voice. He slipped on his shoes and made for the door with his car keys in his hand. He seemed suddenly very young to her: she tried to cherish his vulnerability, but could see him only as callow, rather tiresome in his sudden anxiety to be gone. He looked different in his dark grey professional suit and maroon tie, like an actor playing a role for which he was ill equipped. She could not believe the public would take him seriously in the part, yet she knew he was quite successful. Perhaps this was the reality, and her image of him as lover the deception.

He turned reluctantly, then kissed her on the forehead. The physical contact brought them closer emotionally, but only for the moment it lasted. 'Why is he coming, anyway?' he said. A small worry gnawed in the recesses of his mind.

She shrugged. 'How should I know? It was his sergeant who arranged the time. He's coming too; he sounded like one of your English yeomen. Very sturdy. Very reassuring. Except to a Frenchwoman: Agincourt hasn't the same context for us.'

'Didn't he say what this Lambert fellow wanted to talk about?'

'No. He said it was usual to talk to the next of kin after a death.'

'Not for a Superintendent.'

'We didn't discuss the rank.' She gave him a sharp little smile and he was gone, his blue Sierra roaring swiftly out of earshot, as if he wanted to be well away from the place before the police came. She smiled a little indulgently after him, no longer irritated, merely amused by his childish unease at the approach of the law.

The death had now been officially noted as murder. Neither of them knew that yet.

CHAPTER EIGHT

For senior CID men, there are few better sources of preliminary information than the Desk-Sergeant at the local nick. Lambert was making use of this facility.

'So he lives rough the whole time?'

'Winter and summer. I think occasionally he

75

gets help from someone at the vicarage or the RC presbytery, but clergymen can be quite reticent about those they help. The best clergymen.' Sergeant Johnson made the qualification in sturdy defence of his agnosticism.

'His real name can't be Wino Willy.'

'He's universally known as that now.' Johnson was the opposite of Sergeant Hook: thin-faced, eager, so mobile he seemed to find it difficult to keep still. He shot from his chair as though forcibly ejected, extracted a file from the furthest of three cabinets in ten seconds. He knew the information already, but one needed to be sure and official for a Superintendent.

'Arthur James Harrison,' he said.

'So he's not even Willy really,' said Lambert inconsequentially. The removal of a man's name in the interests of alliteration seemed one more small cruelty visited by an uncaring world upon its flotsam.

'He had a short period in hospital two years ago. Appendix. They cleaned him up. Cut his hair and shaved him. All over, presumably.'

'How long was he in hospital?'

Johnson turned over a page of the file and raised his too-mobile eyebrows. 'Five days.'

'Five days! And discharged back to that! What time of year?' He knew he was being outraged where he should have been non-committal. The swift turnround of patients was one way in which the National Health Service could show itself as efficient in these days of cuts and threatened cuts. He had enough political problems with the Law and Order lobby without looking for more.

'End of August. He discharged himself.' Sergeant Johnson hoped the issue of this information did not sound like a rebuke. Well, it was not after all so irrelevant. Lambert was building up a picture of the man who might just have seen a murder. Or might just have committed it: but he did not believe that. This killing was too carefully arranged to look like suicide by one who must have more motive than poor Arthur James Harrison seemed to have.

'Never mind the file, Jack. Tell me what you know about him beyond that.' So the Superintendent had remembered even his nickname, though he had not spoken to him for two years. Sergeant Johnson was gratified despite himself. Setting aside his twin disadvantages of high rank and CID designation, Lambert did not seem a bad bloke.

'He was divorced eleven years ago. His wife kept the house. He lived in a flat with his son for a while. The son was killed in a car accident six years ago. Front seat passenger. I was there when the firemen cut him out.' Johnson stared at the row of pigeonholes on the wall, his face stilled for a moment with the

77

recollected horror.

'Has he been living rough since then?'

'More or less. That was when he gave up his job. He saw the boy buried, then disappeared for two or three months.

'What was his job?'

'Teacher at the local grammar school; comprehensive, now. Good in his day. Very good, I believe. Inspector Steele reckons he got his son into Cambridge.'

'Subject?'

'History.' Johnson turned back to the beginning of the file. Lambert saw a sharp black and white photograph of an eager, intelligent face. A vanished man. 'An MA. I seem to remember he was writing a book. Never got finished, I suppose. He used to lecture for the WEA at one time. My wife went. Said he was fascinating on Oliver Cromwell.' Like most policemen in the humbler ranks, he was half proud of his wife's erudition and initiative, half threatened by her venture into the exotic world of adult education.

Lambert was grateful for the picture he was building up. He would have to question this half-crazed man whom life had so reduced. He might even have to bring him forward as an important witness: he shuddered at the thought. 'How bad is he? Mentally, I mean.'

Sergeant Johnson pursed his lips. 'The trick-cyclists would no doubt be able to pin some sort of label on him. If they could get at him. I suppose in the old days he might have been committed at some stage. Nowadays, he's left alone, as long as he keeps quiet.'

'Has he had any treatment?'

'Nothing worth the name. Three days' observation a year or so after his wife died. "Severe depression" is all the file says—covers a multitude of sins. Discharged himself after one session of electric shock therapy. Can't say I blame him.'

'Any history of violence?' Lambert asked the question very quietly, but both knew the implications.

'None whatsoever. I haven't seen Willy for three or four years now, but PC Robertson, whose patch it is, says he wouldn't hurt a fly. Rather the reverse, in fact: he has a great reputation for being able to charm the local wildlife. Small animals and birds seem to find him no threat at all and come to sit at his feet. If he holds on another year or two now that even the Tories have gone "green", he'll be transformed from vagrant to conservationist.'

'Human relationships?'

'None to speak of. Kids seem to find him as gentle and attractive as animals do, but these days their mothers snatch them away from strange men. Understandable. Once or twice he's been seen picking bilberries or blackberries with kids on the hills, perfectly innocently I'm sure. Usually he's alone; he seems to avoid human contact whenever he can.'

'Alcoholic?'

'Difficult to say. Unless they cause trouble, we don't see much of them.'

'Meths?'

'It's possible. There's no mention of him buying meths in the file, but he's never given us much trouble, so we've never investigated him much.'

Lambert wondered why he was glad that this did not sound like the profile of a man who would commit premeditated violence. It could hardly be sympathy for that wild figure he had glimpsed so briefly in flight. Such a murderer would have provided a quick, tidy solution, the sort of efficient statistic beloved of Chief Constables. Was he genuinely sympathetic towards this rather tragic underdog? Or was he pleased to have a more complex crime to investigate, relishing the interlocking puzzle he might have to disconnect among those who had been closest to Stanley Freeman?

'Will he be easy to interrogate, Jack?'

Johnson smiled: a daring reaction to a Superintendent, but his nickname had just been used again. 'Sooner you than me, sir. Robertson says he's got worse over the years. Just runs away when he can. How far his son's death sent him over the edge into real madness is anyone's guess. But he's gone wilder since, probably lost all human contact. There's one thing, sir.' For the first time in their exchange, chirpy 'Jack' Johnson looked uncertain about how to proceed with his senior.

'Well?'

'Well, I don't think I'd bring him in here to question him, sir. We had him in about a burglary two years ago—nothing to do with him, and I don't think he'd seen anything. But he was like a frightened animal in a cage. He wouldn't say a word.'

Lambert had already had the same thought, but he said, 'Thanks. Where does he hang out?'

'One place you know of. He seems to have been using that old summerhouse on the edge of the Lydon Hall grounds since the house was empty. I think in summer he sometimes just sleeps under the stars. But Robertson says there's an old sheepcote, disused now, on the edge of the moor; he uses that sometimes. He comes into the town occasionally for supplies, but you might get more out of him on his own ground.'

Lambert walked thoughtfully to his own car, revolving how he might best approach a damaged mind about the most horrifying of human crimes. The man was connected with this death in some way, he was sure. He began to wonder about contacts between Wino Willy and his suspects.

CHAPTER NINE

At precisely two o'clock, Denise Freeman watched the big Vauxhall ease through the gates and park discreetly beside her own car.

The two big men who came unhurriedly towards the house automatically took in their surroundings. Observation was by this time instinctive, but long experience had taught them not to deduce too much too early. They saw a long, low, modern bungalow; as they were not familiar with estate agency language, 'ranch-style' was not the adjective either of them would have used. Lambert saw with interest how the carefully trained wistaria was just beginning to frame the rectangular inset of the front door and its adjoining windows, how clematis clambered in abundance over climbing roses, how the circular bed in the front lawn combined geraniums, tagetes and lobelia in parkland precision. 'Paid gardener,' he muttered to Hook as a speculation.

His sergeant was peering into the large segment of rear garden visible past the side of the house. The swimming pool looked blue and inviting against the surrounding green, the garish red-hot pokers and more muted phlox looked like a backdrop from *Ideal Home*. 'Not a vegetable in sight,' he said with disgust.

Denise Freeman could not know she had

made a bad beginning with Sergeant Hook. She opened the front door with a bright smile, moderated it a little in deference to her widowed status, and held out her hand to his chief. 'Superintendent Lambert? Denise Freeman. Delighted to meet you.'

In the complex relationships of interviewer and interviewed, the shaking of hands did not normally figure, but Lambert took the proffered hand with only a momentary hesitation. It was small and warm, the grip firm enough to imply confidence, the contact brief enough to maintain a degree of formality. Perhaps the information he brought would shake this composure; or perhaps she already knew; the majority of homicides were still domestic.

'Will this take long?' she said. Her smile implied that she would be patient, but they must not impinge too harshly upon the privacy of grief.

'It might. It all depends how much you can tell us. I think we should sit down somewhere.' They were still standing in the hall; if he was going to give her an unpleasant shock, he didn't want her fainting upon them. But at this moment she looked a very controlled lady.

'I thought we might sit in the garden. It's warm enough. Would you like some tea?' Lambert assented, trying not to see Bert Hook's ill-concealed gratification behind their hostess. Hook had never been known to refuse a cup of tea, and his axiom of 'the bourgeois the better' would add to the delight of this context. Coffee from the Crown's silver jug this morning, and now tea here: criminal investigation was looking up.

Denise Freeman led them through the bungalow to where a crazy-paved patio overlooked lawn, pool, manicured garden and oak trees beyond. Lambert was puzzled by the vaguely familiar air of a spot he had never seen before. Then he realized it was a small-scale, modernized version of the more grandiose view from the terrace at the rear of Lydon Hall, where he had stood on the previous day, speculating about murder and its possible witness in the arboretum.

Here there were cups, saucers and plates upon a solid wooden table. So she had planned this, half expecting a prolonged exchange and seeking to keep its social context as low-key as possible. They seated themselves on garden furniture more opulent than many lounge suites and prepared for the ceremony of tea. Bert Hook had already decided that the china was more 'refined' than even the Crown's. It was a favourite adjective of his, pronounced with a curl of the lip: 'refinement' had been held out to a 'fifties Barnardo's boy as the ultimate in morality.

He was not disappointed by Denise Freeman's arrival with silver tea service. The dark pink sleeveless dress set off the slim brown arms and calves to perfection, as she had known it would. It was modestly buttoned to the neck. The neat lace trimmings and simple low-heeled sandals were elegant yet unpretentious. With tray in hand, she looked to Bert Hook very ladylike. It was an adjective that did not prevent him from reserving his judgements: his upbringing had brought him into contact with many ladies who had given him hard times.

'Is this usual? I already spoke to a policewoman on the night Stanley died.' With only the slight hesitation over tenses to suggest that English was not her first language, Denise broached the question which had worried her in the hours since she had taken Hook's phone call and accepted this meeting.

'Yes. The Coroner's Officer collects the body and arranges for the next of kin to be informed.' Lambert was in no hurry to dispense information. Once foul play is established, spouses are always prime suspects, whether as direct agents of death or accessories; he was content to study this one carefully. Was she anticipating his disclosure? She seemed to be prepared for something, but that might be no more than the reaction of an intelligent woman to a visit from the CID. Even to an eye trained to spot disclosures, her body language gave nothing away. Her hand as she poured the tea was firm enough, her voice steady as the poise of her head as she handed the delicate crockery into the large, careful hands of her visitors. For a woman suddenly widowed, she seemed unnaturally calm, but this kind of control was not an unusual reaction in those confronting official functionaries in the days after bereavement; sometimes people did not feel the full impact of death until after the funeral.

'I should begin by offering our sympathy, and apologizing for intruding at a time like this,' said Lambert.

The wide, still lips permitted themselves a small smile. 'Thank you. And why do you?' she said.

'What do you know about your husband's death?'

'That his body was found at Lydon Hall on the night before last. That his suicide appeared to have been planned carefully.' The word 'suicide' dropped from her lips naturally enough, with no hesitation, and rather less emotion than most widows would have shown.

'What can you tell us about your husband's movements on that night?'

The dark eyes flashed to Lambert's face, but he was ready for her; he had done this too often for his impassivity to be disturbed. She was looking at the table as she replied, 'Almost nothing. He didn't tell me about his appointments.' It was curious: the bitterness with which she spoke was overlaid with regret by the end of the sentence. She brushed a fly angrily away as it threatened to land on her saucer, as if banishing with it any display of weakness.

'When was the last time you saw him?' He hesitated a little over the end of the question before omitting the last, brutal word.

But she understood and added it for him. 'Alive, you mean? I identified the body at nine o'clock yesterday morning.' Again there was a strange combination, the harshness of the statement delivered with a tenderness that was a strange setting for it. It was the apparently contradictory emotions which interested Lambert. Someone dissimulating in these circumstances might well act out either grief or indifference, but they would hardly go for a combination of the two. In his experience, those wishing to deceive went hard for a single effect. He cast aside compassionate tact in favour of more directness.

'Yes, Mrs Freeman. I need to know when you last saw your husband alive.' As if noting the change of mood, Bert Hook flicked over the last page of his notebook and prepared to record the detail. She glanced sideways at him for a moment, and Lambert saw more clearly the dark patches beneath the eyes, the beginnings of crow's feet at their sides. It might have been a moment of fear; but in the shock which follows bereavement, any small invasion of privacy can be a source of resentment and alarm. Innocence as well as guilt has its secrets, and strives to protect them.

She turned her attention back to Lambert with a quick, impatient jerk of her head, so that the neat switch of jet-black hair swung briefly behind her neck. Before she spoke, he knew she had had enough of this preliminary fencing.

'I am not used to the ways of the British police. But I don't think it can be usual for the wife—the widow—to be visited and questioned by a Superintendent.' She realized with a spurt of surprise that she was using Simon Hapgood's view of things. But she gave nothing away; if the trace of a French accent touched her pronunciation of Lambert's rank, she could not after all have been expected to have used the word much in the past. 'What exactly is going on?'

Lambert sighed a little, gathering his resources. He would watch her like a hawk, learning whatever he could from her reactions, but the revelation of murder to a wife was not a moment to savour. Always assuming, of course, that it would come as a surprise.

'Mrs Freeman, did your husband give you any reason to suppose he might be planning to take his own life?'

He had her attention now, her eyes widening slowly in a whitening face. She was ahead of him.

'None at all.'

'Suicide without previous threats to call attention to distress is unusual, though not unknown. Your husband had no serious disease? Or fear of any disease?'

She shook her head, anxious now for him to get to the fact that she had already guessed at.

'Business worries?' He tried not to notice the affluence all around them as he spoke and she rejected the preposterous idea. He was not sure whether he was prolonging the moment through a desire to allow her the time to assimilate brutal fact, or from some baser desire to study her reactions, to assess in these long seconds of stress how genuine was her surprise.

'You may or may not be familiar with an organization called EXIT. It exists to help people who wish to end their own lives. Usually in cases of incurable illness, where people wish to avoid long periods of what they see as hopeless medication.'

She nodded, impatient to get to the end. Perhaps, he thought suddenly, she was imagining that he was about to reveal the identity of her husband's murderer. If so, he would have given a good deal to know who she thought was guilty; for a moment, her face was sick with apprehension.

She said, 'I don't think my husband was a member of EXIT. He never mentioned it.'

'And you can think of no one who might have helped him to kill himself in this way?'

'Superintendent, this is ridiculous.' This time there was no trace of accent on the word; perhaps her impatience carried her forward, like a stammerer who loses his impediment with increased animation. 'Stanley wasn't that sort of man. The one thing that amazed me about his death is that he should have taken his own life.'

Lambert finished drinking his tea, set the delicate china carefully back on the garden table, and braced himself for his disclosure. She had given no sign of being devastated by her husband's death, so that he could not think his revelation would cause her too much anguish. Unless, of course, she had killed him herself, in which case the sudden knowledge that the police were aware of the crime would be most unwelcome.

'Mrs Freeman, I have to tell you that we are now inclined to the view that your husband's death was murder.'

'Inclined to the view?' In this moment of stress, she picked up half-ironically the very periphrasis he had despised in himself. He caught Hook looking at her curiously, trying to assess whether this was the illogicality of shock or a deliberate evasion of that darkest of crimes which had followed the phrase.

'Let us say that we are convinced that Mr Freeman was murdered by person or persons as yet unknown, and will produce evidence to that effect at the inquest. We are now in the first stages of a murder inquiry. That is why we have come to see you now, as next of kin to the deceased.'

'And chief suspect!' she said, very quietly. She put the empty teacups tidily upon the tray, as if testing for herself how steadily she could move. There was no vibration, from crockery or teaspoons. Lambert's close scrutiny gave him no clue as to whether the news of murder came as a surprise or not to her. Hook had already marked her down as 'Very cool under fire'.

'We don't have suspects,' said Lambert, with a smile to offer the reassurance she did not seem to need. 'We assemble whatever facts we can from those nearest the crime.' It was a summary of his advice to young CID men.

'Or we suspect everyone,' said Denise Freeman with a dry smile.

'That is sometimes how the public sees it,' acknowledged Lambert with an answering smile. He knew he must beware of the respect that always became a temptation when he met intellects wishing to cross swords with his own. 'The simplest procedure for us is usually to eliminate as suspects all those people who could not have committed the crime. Often they can show that they were in a different place at the time of the murder.'

'Those who have an alibi,' she said.

'If you like,' he smiled. 'It's not a legal concept, but it will serve.'

'What time was Stanley killed?' It was the first time she had voiced the thought, and he caught a moment of abhorrence and regret, genuine unless she was the subtlest of actresses.

'That I cannot tell you at present. We know when the body was found. The post-mortem will give us further information.'

'Stomach contents,' she said with a shudder. She was looking, grey-faced and unseeing, at a sparrow on the edge of the pool. For a moment, he thought she was going to be sick with the nausea of her husband's mutilation.

He said unhelpfully, because he could think of nothing else, 'You know about post-mortems?'

'A little. A long time ago, I used to be a biochemist.'

'When we have questioned everyone, I think we shall be able to pinpoint the time of the crime quite exactly.' He was glad she was too upset for the moment to press him on that 'everyone': he had no intention of revealing the present paucity of witnesses. 'What I need to know now is where you were for the whole of Wednesday evening.'

Bert Hook, who had made a covert note about her knowledge of chemistry, now flicked over a page of his notebook ostentatiously. Whether or not she was a grieving widow, she was now a murder suspect. If the thought made her a little nervous, that could be to the advantage of her interrogators.

She said calmly, 'Starting when?'

'When did you last see Mr Freeman?'

'About three in the afternoon.' The reply came so promptly that she must have given it prior thought; but it would be strange if she had not.

'Do you know where he ate his evening meal?'

Her dark eyes flashed back a quick, hostile look. Perhaps she knew his information must come from the post-mortem and the ignominious investigation of her husband's stomach; or perhaps she felt some implication about their domestic arrangements.

'No. Stanley ate out. He often did.' One could derive a world of speculation from the manner of the curt understatement; Lambert did not have to, for she chose to go on unprompted. 'Superintendent, if you are going to question Stanley's employees, you will no doubt find this out anyway. Ours was not a perfect marriage. Stanley and I have not been close for years.' Lambert had met the phrase so often: it covered arrangements which ranged from an active but joyless marital bed, through separate rooms, to a malevolent mutual hostility which surprised only in that it could be contained within four walls. If the Freemans' marriage proved relevant to the case, much sordid detail might tumble out in due course; for the moment, he was content to record the beginnings of a motive.

As if she followed his thoughts, Denise Freeman said calmly, 'That does not mean I killed him, or wanted him dead. It seems incredible that Stanley could be murdered. But as I said when you came, it seemed incredible to me that he should have killed himself. I don't know which is worse.' For a moment her voice broke and she seemed near tears, but she recovered so fast that he was left wondering if it was a contrived effect. 'I hope you get whoever did this. And quickly. Stanley didn't deserve this.' There was bitterness now, probably against the killer, but possibly just the normal emptiness of the bereaved for the missed opportunities of the last, barren years. In all, she was remarkably composed in the circumstances. Calm enough for a murderer? Lambert saw Hook making the same cool assessment over his notebook: they had worked together too long for his thought processes not to be transparent to his chief.

Lambert said, 'Thank you for being so open with us at this difficult time. You will find you did the wise thing. Now, can you tell us if Mr Freeman had a relationship with any member of his staff that might be thought abnormal?'

In his search for tact, his phrasing had become clumsy and he knew it. She glanced at him with what he could have sworn was amusement, then gave thought to her reply. 'George Robson had his own reasons for resentment, which he'll no doubt tell you about himself. I suspect Emily Godson had, too, but I wouldn't know what they were.'

She paused, as if to estimate the effects she had made by these intriguing suggestions about the operations of Freeman Estates. Then she said, 'I'm sure there was something between Stanley and Jane Davidson, but I couldn't tell you what. I doubt whether he was bedding her, though it never pays to underestimate the naïvety of the young. But she seemed to have some hold over him.'

Even among widows who seemed to have much less regret for their husbands' passing than Denise Freeman, Lambert had never met this degree of composure. He said, 'What about your own movements after your husband had left?'

'I was here until about a quarter to seven. I was in the garden for an hour or so, then I made myself a meal.'

'You were alone throughout this time?' It was not by any means a key period, but perhaps she did not know that.

'Yes. There was a phone call from the office inquiring after Stanley. You could check on that.'

'What time would that be?'

'I couldn't be certain. I should think about five.'

'And who made the call?'

For a moment, she looked disconcerted.

Perhaps she had not expected this level of detail in the questioning. A murderess of course would know how irrelevant this time was.

'Simon Hapgood, I think.' Strange, that: a woman as precise as she had been in her earlier replies would hardly be uncertain about the identity of a caller. Lambert waited for Hook to record the name laboriously before he went on.

'And where did you go at a quarter to seven?'

'Out for the evening. To the cinema in Tewkesbury.' She looked at him boldly, almost as if she knew she was trying to establish an alibi. This was a classic one when someone was trying to cover a longish period of time: perhaps she knew that.

To disconcert her a little, he switched the questioner, so that he could concentrate on her reactions. 'Sergeant Hook will need to record the detail of this.' He gestured towards his subordinate, and Bert Hook took up the questioning without hesitation. He seemed deliberately ponderous; Lambert himself was never sure on these occasions whether it was his natural manner or the role of sedate country bobby he chose to play. Certainly it was an effective disguise for the shrewd brain within that stolid exterior.

'Who accompanied you to the cinema, Mrs Freeman?'

'No one.'

'You went alone?' Bert's modest surprise made it sound like a moral outrage.

'Yes. I often do. It's years since I went with Stanley.' And now you never will again. Three very different minds shared the same thought as Hook wrote.

'You drove to Tewkesbury?'

'Yes.'

'And which street did you park in?'

'In the public car park near the cinema. It's free in the evenings.' And much more difficult to check on than a street, where householders will often remember the colour and make of a car parked for a whole evening, especially in summer. Lambert thought that Denise Freeman appreciated this as fully as Bert Hook.

'What car do you drive, Mrs Freeman?'

'It's a green Volvo.' Green could easily be mistaken for blue against a low evening sun; Lambert toyed with the idea while she gave Hook the details of year and registration number. Many women would not have known these without checking: Denise Freeman was as effortlessly accurate as a well-prepared witness. He wondered if that was exactly what she was.

'Did you see anyone who could confirm that you were in the cinema during the evening?'

Perhaps her negative came a little too quickly. But she was an intelligent woman, and might well by this time be anticipating the line of Hook's methodical interrogation.

'And the film you saw?'

'The Last Emperor.'

She gave Hook in turn the starting time, the duration, the stars and a detailed résumé of the plot of the film. Lambert, listening and watching carefully, found it impossible to say whether or not this was a prepared performance. He was certain by the end of it that she had indeed seen the film. There was nothing as yet to prove that she had seen it on Wednesday night. But then the innocent were never looking at the time for people to substantiate their accounts.

Lambert, seeking to ruffle a calm that now seemed quite unnatural, said, 'Your husband had taken valium in the hours before his death. Perhaps immediately before. There is no evidence in his medical records of it being prescribed for him.' He left it there, hoping she would respond without more questions, and in a moment she did.

'They were probably mine,' she said. 'I haven't used them for months.' Not since before Simon, she thought. 'Stanley took one or two of them, occasionally. I think he thought I didn't know.' She was genuinely distressed with the bleakness of it all, but she showed nothing beyond a small tightening of the muscles around her mouth.

Lambert watched Hook recording the

98

detail, wondering if she would show any more obvious emotion when all this came out at the inquest. Then he switched his ground again. 'What do you know of a man called Wino Willy?'

This time he had certainly surprised her. He found himself wishing the coal-black eyes were just a little lighter, for he had the idea he might then have distinguished between bewilderment and alarm in them, as he could not do now. He had expected a blank ignorance of Willy's existence, perhaps because her tight self-possession seemed so much the antithesis of his disintegration, but she said, 'Yes, I know him. Or used to. When I came here and was struggling with the language, he was one of the few people who spoke fluent French. It is quite a long time ago.' She stared out at the end of the garden, recalling a different world. 'He even knew and liked Racine,' she said inconsequentially. 'Not many English do.'

' *"Je l'ai trop aimé pour ne le point haïr,"* ' said Lambert before he could stop himself. It was pure vanity, and he regretted it immediately.

She looked at him and said, 'Yes. "I have loved him too much not to hate him a little." *Andromaque.* Not what I would have expected from a British policeman. Even a Superintendent.'

Lambert caught Hook enjoying his
99

discomfiture and hastened to end an interview that had almost run its course. 'Have you seen Willy recently?'

She hesitated a moment before she said, 'Only in the distance on the common sometimes. He still knows me, I think.' Perhaps for her, too, there was a small, illogical vanity, in the thought that that ravaged personality should still register her presence when it had obliterated others.

Lambert said, 'We appreciate that this must be a great strain for you, Mrs Freeman, at a time like this. Thank you for being so helpful.' She seemed calm enough again, too calm perhaps for a grieving widow. She was looking at him keenly now, trying to detect any irony in his last words. 'Perhaps you can appreciate that we are now investigating the most serious of all crimes, so that your information is vital to us. I have to ask you now if you can think of anyone who might have reason to harm your husband.'

He was sure this time that there was fear in her face, as she looked suddenly full into his. She could not quite control the movement of those slim, ballerina's arms. Her eyes moved from him to the attentive Hook, then up to the innocent sky, where white clouds cruised slow and high against the blue. Her eyes closed; her uplifted face, with its dark hair dropping away behind it like a schoolgirl's, looked both serious and innocent. Her voice when it came was very low, but perfectly clear.

'I've wondered about other women, of course. I don't think there can be anything that would have led to murder, or I should have known about it.' She said it with the unconscious arrogance of a superior intellect assessing an inferior one. 'It's someone in the firm. It must be.'

Or in the immediate family, thought Bert Hook as he shut his notebook.

She watched them go, standing calm and slender, her dress bright pink against the dark rectangle of the door behind her, as if she were posed for a painter. She stayed there until long after the big Vauxhall had disappeared, until its sound had purred softly away into silence.

She sat in an armchair for a full minute, wondering how effectively she had deceived her visitors about her movements on the night of the murder. Then she picked up the phone to ring Simon Hapgood.

CHAPTER TEN

In the oldest industrial quarter of Gloucester, a woman stared at the sky.

It was the same sky that so brilliantly overmantled Denise Freeman's manicured half-acre, but through the square north window with its broken sash, the blue was less

101

brilliant and hopeful. The Victorian working conditions which had placed these mean terraces near to the factories and their twelve-hour days had long since gone, but Victorian grime clung obstinately, despite the spasmodic local improvements of landlord and local authority. Dusk seemed to arrive a little earlier here, as if the climate itself reminded the citizens that they had less reason to trust the future than others outside this shrinking area of decay.

The woman was five years younger than Denise Freeman; she looked five years older. Denise's straight and lustrous black hair owed a little to bottled help, but the effect was complete and compelling. The peroxide used on this head was less comprehensive in its effects, so that there was tell-tale darkness at the roots and the occasional spot at the ends where a close observer might see blonde becoming grey. Perhaps the make-up on the face had been a little too thick, the eye-shadow a little too heavy. It was impossible to tell now. For the woman had been crying for a long time, not with the noisy, uncontrollable sobs that convulse and then pass, but with the slow, hopeless tears of despair.

On the high mantelpiece of the old fireplace, she looked again at the envelope in Stanley's neat round writing. 'Ms Margot Jones'. The title was a little joke between them, one of Stanley's small pamperings she

102

had enjoyed so much, her tiny link with the feminism which had passed her by without other trace. This month's cheque was still inside: even through her grief, a practical voice within her gave ignoble thanks for that. An outsider would have seen Stanley Freeman's recompense as mean enough for what the relationship gave him, but there was a certain delicacy in the method of payment. The money arrived like a regular allowance to a favoured, virtuous child, with no suggestion of the price for services rendered which might have been implied by cash exchanging hands at their meetings.

Like the wife she had never seen, this other woman of Stanley Freeman's made tea, but in her case it was the dull ritual of the only therapy she could offer herself. She took the half-empty packet from the shelf in the tiny kitchenette, lit the gas under the aluminium kettle, dropped a tea-bag straight into the one mug which had no crack. For Stanley, she would have got out the pretty earthenware teapot, and cups and saucers; what was the use of bothering for one?

Two years they had had. Two years which began with a pick-up in a pub and developed to an affection, an easiness with each other, even to something like love. They had even begun to make small, tentative plans. She was learning to type on the machine he had brought as a write-off from work. He would get her a cottage in a small town away from here and she, with her new skills and his help, would find work, respectable work at last. She looked at the typewriter beneath the plastic cover, and the tears began again from the ducts she had thought must surely be dry.

The kettle spat steam and water for thirty seconds before she registered it. She poured the water into her beaker, tipped the last milk from the bottle, watched the first flecks of its souring float briefly on the top of the darkening water. Then she sat in the armchair to torment herself again with the evening edition of the local newspaper.

TRAGIC DEATH OF OLDFORD ESTATE AGENT. The headline was a little cramped, the item hurriedly accommodated in the bottom right-hand corner of the front page. The hard-pressed editor had not been able to obtain Stanley's age, and would not guess at it in the case of a local luminary. The account mentioned that Stanley was childless, but left a widow. There was of course no mention of Margot. How could there be? Yet her absence from this brief account of his death seemed to diminish her place in his life, as if that had after all been only one more of the deceptions that had been practised so often upon her. She read again to the end. 'Foul play is not suspected.' The police release had not said anything so definite, but the eager young reporter had unearthed enough details of the apparent suicide for his editor to back this modest speculation. Next day's edition would blaze murder in thick black headlines, but Margot Jones could not know that yet.

She stared at the familiar phrase. It meant suicide, didn't it? For a bleak moment, she wished worldly-wise Stanley was at her shoulder to confirm her interpretation. So he had done this on Wednesday night, when he should have been coming back to her. But he couldn't have. Wouldn't have. Not on the night he kept for her. She could not accept that Stanley could have committed suicide. A heart attack perhaps: sometimes in her bad moments she had thought that their world might end in that. But he would not top himself; not on their night together, certainly. Suddenly, it was very important to her that he could not have killed himself. If he had done that when he should have been coming to her, then all of it had been false, and she was back in the nightmare he had gently dispersed for her over the last few months. Sipping the scalding tea, she found it tainted with salt tears.

It was there in print: it must be so. Then in her misery there came back to her a picture she had thought long since lost. It was of the father who had left them in Swansea, years before she changed Maggie to Margot and moved out herself. He was saying, as she remembered now he often did, that you could not believe everything you read in the papers. It had meant nothing to a child, like the rest of his drink-laden diatribes. Now it came back to her like a biblical pronouncement. That must be it. The newspaper, unthinkably, was wrong. She rocked herself backwards and forwards, cradling the beaker close to her breast.

She must put it right. The thought became a palliative for her grief. In the two hours of her steady, silent tears, she had confronted the abyss. Before Stanley, she had lived through a series of desperate affairs, each offering brief hope of a lasting attachment, each shorter than the last. Stanley, finding her in a pub, had thought her an easy prospect. After that first, clumsy coupling, there had emerged from their dual loneliness an affection which had massaged a slow confidence back into both of them. Now he was gone, and the path was opening again to drinking, to the joyless sex which was the only currency she could offer, perhaps to eventual prostitution.

She could not formulate the words even in her thoughts, but the notion sat in her consciousness like a sullen dog and would not be ignored. She must explain that Stanley had been coming to see her last night. That because of that, he could never have committed suicide. It was her grasp upon integrity.

Her first thought was to visit the newspaper. Then even she realized that this could not be right. It would have to be the police. She had never in her life gone voluntarily to them. To do so now in the extreme of her distress and physical collapse took a courage which women from a different background would never comprehend. It took an hour to nerve herself to go. An hour of fear, but an hour in which she became more sure what she must do. She owed it to Stanley: to their relationship.

She found the gin bottle in the bottom of the wardrobe. It had only been a quarter full, and she had almost finished it while she waited for Stanley on Wednesday. It was curious now to think that she had been only disappointed, not fearful, as the possibility that he could not come back to her grew into a certainty. There was a bare half-inch in the bottom of the bottle; she finished it now with the tonic she had so carefully preserved for Stanley. Then she washed herself carefully and put on the green two-piece costume Stanley had paid for and so admired. She brushed her hair vigorously, the first energetic movement she had made since she had come in with the paper and read the news.

In the mirror, she saw a drawn face which seemed to belong to someone older and more tragic than Margot Jones could ever be. She wanted to go without make-up to the police station, for all the obscure memories of puberty and adolescence were insisting that this was respectable. But the lined face, still puffed from weeping, seemed too vulnerable and revealing. She put a light base on the white cheeks, trying to rub a little life into them so that the colouring would not seem so obstinately artificial. She put on lipstick, a little more than she intended, changing the face in the mirror a little nearer to the mask she had hoped to avoid. In the second drawer of the battered tallboy, she sought the gloves she had not worn for years, those childhood guarantees of respectability. There was only one there. She did not possess a hat.

She crept quietly downstairs, not wanting the landlady to know her errand; she could not know that the old woman had been questioned thoroughly earlier in the day. In the dingy hall, she took a last deep breath, then made for the outside world and the terrors of authority. Her hand was six inches from the handle of the front door when the knocker crashed harshly on the outside, not two feet from her face. The noise was clattering still in her head when she opened the door.

She stepped back instinctively, flinching before the dark blue uniform, its buttons unnaturally bright after the gloom within. The constable took in the stained, flowered wallpaper, the scratched brown paint, the hall carpet fraying into holes, the smell of old cabbage and older dog. Delicacy would bring no returns from the people here, he decided.

'Margaret Jones?' She nodded dumbly.

'We're contacting the associates of a Stanley Gordon Freeman. We have reason to believe you may be able to help us.'

She had never known that ridiculous middle name. For an absurd moment before she remembered, she thought she would tease him with it when they met again.

The policeman stepped inside the door and she retreated before him, nodding fearfully. Was it an offence to change Margaret to Margot, she wondered.

He caught the gin upon her breath. 'You'd better tell us everything you can. You can talk to us here or come to the station, it's up to you,' he said aggressively. He was due off in twenty minutes.

It was the first time she had realized that he was not alone. She looked from the white car with its blue trim to the house windows with their faces which did not trouble to conceal themselves. Then she turned hopelessly back upstairs, transformed from volunteer to police quarry.

Even her one small bravery had been denied to her.

CHAPTER ELEVEN

Audrey Robson looked through the new double glazing, down the long back garden, to the gate where George had recently disappeared. Was he feeling as guilty as she did? She had seen no sign of it.

She had tried many times in the last two days to be sorry about Stanley Freeman's death. Unsuccessfully. Phrases she had thought forgotten had come strangely back to her. And with the phrases there had returned each time a strange, a ludicrous image of herself, with strong adolescent bosom flattened for much of the play beneath a breastplate, playing Bolingbroke in *Richard II*. It must be thirty-five years ago now, long before these enlightened days when boys were brought in to play men's parts in school plays. She had stood sturdily, feet astride on the rickety stage of the Girls' High School, her height and rich contralto securing for her the masculine roles she secretly desired.

When Richard's murderer had stood before her expecting reward in the last scene of their severely cut version, she had struck a pious attitude and declaimed,

They love not poison that do poison need,
Nor do I thee. Though I did wish him dead,
I hate the murderer, love him murdered.

All through the day these half-forgotten words
had come insistently back to her, until they
had formed a mocking chorus to all the dutiful
pangs of regret she had tried to feel. Stanley
Freeman was no Richard of Bordeaux; he was
a despicable little crook who had frustrated
George for twenty years, that was all. And
through George, her. She could not get away
from the fact that in that time she had often
wished him dead. Ever since that initial
treachery all those years ago . . .

She set the last dish upon the drainer,
peeled off her rubber gloves, and inspected
her hands at the window in the last rays of the
setting sun. It was a flattering, old-master light,
gilding everything in roseate warmth,
disguising from its low angle the wrinkles a
more brilliant illumination would have
revealed. But they were good hands, not so
very different from those which had struck
stage attitudes all those years ago. The pale
pink varnish on the long nails looked in this
glowing light exactly as it had in the
advertisement.

She went into the lounge at the front of the
house. It was darker here, but she resisted
artificial light as the dusk seemed to creep
prematurely over the heavy furniture. Perhaps

111

it was just a psychological reluctance to admit the departure of another summer day. More likely it was a long-thrown effect from her childhood on a farm in the Yorkshire Dales. There, the soft light of the oil lamps had been allowed only in the last of the twilight, and early starts on long summer days had meant that the lamps were only a prelude to retiring for the night. Light there was not for reading: on a farm that was the worst form of sloth. 'Sitting there with a book in your hand wasting time again, my girl!' they'd say, and she'd start as guiltily as if indulging some solitary vice.

Well, she had moved away a long time ago from that world of exploitation and small, grudgingly conceded privileges; and good riddance to it. George had his faults, but he had taken her away from all that. Cosseted her, in the early years. He never begrudged her good clothes, even now: she looked down at the leather shoes, comfortable despite their heels, and tried not to be proud of the sleek limbs beneath the nylon. In North Yorkshire, those shapely legs would have been channelled with varicose veins by now. It was part of her reaction to those long, lonely trudges to schools and school buses that she rarely walked nowadays, and never stood when she could sit. She liked the dog, but was content to feed him and occasionally fuss him. It was George who walked him, especially in the evenings. Where once he had grumbled, even

112

shamed her into taking her turn, for months now he had accepted the ritual of the evening walk with resignation, even enjoyment.

She supposed it had become a release from the frustrations of the day's work and Stanley Freeman's petty incivilities. Now, with Freeman's death, there might open a new era of increased prosperity and increased satisfaction. Walking Fred might become a relaxed, contrasting part of a nicely balanced day. She might even accompany them occasionally, on evenings like this. She folded her arms beneath the russet cashmere, hugged herself, and tried not to feel the warm, animal satisfaction of a child who has secured some small triumph and thinks the world is hers. Freeman had cheated, and cheated badly. He could not expect to be lamented now. She sank into the heavy flowered cushions and savoured for long minutes the fact that they had done with him for ever.

The clear northern sky moved towards indigo; the room had a soft gloom that seemed a conspirator to her mood. Her sign as she eventually rose to put the lights on was one of pure contentment. She went first to draw the curtains, another habit coming across the long decades from childhood. It was as she pulled the cord and the curtains slid quietly around the big bay that she saw the men.

All sun had gone now; the sober-suited figures, coming steadily up the long path through the front garden, seemed sinister in their silent advance. She had to control an absurd instinct to hide, to pretend that the lightless house was unoccupied. Perhaps that was also a childish legacy.

She went into the spacious hall and firmly switched on the light. When she opened the door, the light behind her illuminated the features of the men, but made all beyond them seem darker. She could scarcely make out the garden; only the sombre outline of the big hawthorn at the gate registered as her pupils strove to focus.

The nearer man was tall and lean, well over six feet. He had dark hair, which crinkled into grey at the temples, and blue, incongruously humorous eyes. 'Mrs Robson? I'm Superintendent Lambert,' he said. He turned towards the slightly shorter and more rotund figure at his side. 'This is Sergeant Hook, who rang your husband earlier.' The Sergeant gave her a small, ceremonial smile: she felt both of them assessing her.

'You'd best come in,' she said, and the Yorkshire she had thought long left behind came leaping out in the words. The men, filling the doorway as they stepped forward, seemed to her like angels of death.

The tall one explained their visit as they walked through a hall which now seemed to her empty, not spacious. Perhaps it was only the guilty feelings she had indulged all day

114

which made his words seem so ominous.

For all he said was, 'It's about Stanley Freeman. We're investigating the circumstances of his death.'

CHAPTER TWELVE

They sat in armchairs big enough to accommodate even their frames with room to spare. It was a comfortable room, slightly old-fashioned perhaps, with its huge, heavy suite, Indian carpet and big tiled fireplace. And none the worse for that thought Bert Hook, still resentful that the Superintendent had refused their third offer of refreshment in the day. He looked past the etchings of nineteenth-century Whitby to the oak corner cupboard with its gleaming brass fittings, and speculated upon its contents.

'It's most unlike George to forget an appointment,' said Audrey Robson as she rejoined them. She carried herself well, walking with poise to the vacant settee between them, as if she were making a stage entrance. Lambert wondered if she had paused outside the door for a moment, gathering her resources to make this effect. The soft cashmere caressed rather than concealed the still shapely breasts, the plaid skirt was modestly long, but her carriage depended on legs he would have had to describe as shapely rather than sturdy: if professionally called upon, of course. She must be around fifty, but she remained attractive without fighting the years. Her carefully coiffured hair was silver, almost white, an agreeable frame for her strong features. It set off the rather large nose and high cheekbones, and deepened the colour of the widely set grey eyes. In the brief interval when she had left the policemen alone, she had applied the lightest of make-up. So her surprise when they arrived had been genuine: she had not been expecting them.

'George is on the common with Fred,' she said. For a moment, the unwelcome possibility of another suspect flashed through their minds. Perhaps she saw it, for she said with a little smile, 'Fred's our dog. George walks him on the common nearly every night at this time. You're privileged he arranged to meet you now. But perhaps you're a little early?'

By this time, it was twenty minutes past the appointed time, but to say so explicitly seemed a criticism. They chatted awkwardly, with Lambert carefully preserving his news that the death was murder until he had Robson present. He began to wish he had accepted the offer of yet more tea. Policemen's small talk is notoriously ineffective, principally because their audiences, waiting for the large talk they know is the real purpose, refuse to join in the game. When Hook gallantly enlarged upon the virtues of housing plots large enough to accommodate decent kitchen gardens, Mrs Robson's polite, half-amused agreements were not the returns to keep a conversational rally going. All three of them were glad to hear the sounds of movement in the rear section of the house. The hiatus was terminated abruptly by the arrival in their midst of a golden labrador. He burst open the unlatched door, circled with whirling tail among the visitors he assumed had come to see him, checked expertly for evidence of food and was disappointed. He had the unerring eye of his breed for a soft touch, for he settled eventually by Bert Hook, set his chin upon the Sergeant's sturdy knee, and fixed soft brown eyes unblinkingly upon the rubicund face above him. 'There's a conversation-stopper!' said Lambert, pleased to imply that they had been in the middle of an animated exchange.

George Robson stood apologetically in the doorway behind him, battered trilby in hand, green anorak unzipped, gumboots unmuddied on this balmy evening. 'Terribly sorry,' he said breathlessly. 'I forgot completely about our appointment until Fred and I were way up beyond the common.'

'I told them it wasn't like you,' said the wife. 'Everything else, including my birthday, but never a business appointment!' Hook, stroking Fred, wondered if she would emerge as one of

117

those middle-aged women charitable towards all human nature except their husbands. It was a side-effect of monogamy which CID investigations seemed often to illustrate, and Hook, who had married late and regarded himself as a novice to the state, found it disturbing. Mrs Robson was looking at her husband with her head slightly on one side, as if estimating the progress of a garden plant and finding it barely satisfactory. Bert was too inexperienced to divine the deeper current of affection, which ran beneath with no surface sign of its existence.

George Robson, having divested himself of his outer garments, subsided into an armchair beside Hook, still panting a little. Lambert reflected that it was as well that he had the dog to give him exercise, for his strong frame was everywhere running a little to fat. Robson was certainly not gross; indeed, he was physically still a powerful man. His wrists and forearms were as strong as a manual worker's, and his deep chest gave him a barrel-like torso. There was an early suggestion of blood pressure in the colour of cheeks that were just too full. Though his small features had no longer the precision of youth, he remained a good-looking man.

'Would you like me to withdraw and leave you alone?' Audrey Robson sounded as though she was recalling them to business after the diversions of Fred. She did not trouble to

118

conceal her pleasure when Lambert said there was no need. Hook was well enough versed in the irregular ways of his chief to raise not even a figurative eyebrow. Wives added another dimension to a husband's portrait, often stripping away the very image the subject was trying to create for himself. Robson sat looking relaxed and untroubled. His spouse's intelligent, unguarded presence might well test the role. If role it was.

'When did you hear of Stanley Freeman's death?' Lambert began. He would take them through all the preliminaries, studying reactions: neither of them seemed very distressed, and that in itself was interesting.

'Late on Wednesday night. We were getting ready for bed when the phone rang. It was Denise Freeman about Stanley's suicide.' Did Robson assert the word with just a touch of self-conscious stress? Lambert allowed a pause to stretch after it, but it was impossible to deduce whether it was a murderer testing the ground or an innocent using the word without subterfuge.

Audrey Robson broke the silence, as if it was painful to her. 'It was twenty past eleven. I had the clock in my hands, adjusting the alarm for an early start in the morning.'

Her husband did not even look at her. He said, 'The police had just left Mrs Freeman's house.'

'She sounded upset?' Lambert wanted to

see how he would react to the deliberately foolish question.

'Of course she did. Wouldn't your wife sound upset, if a policewoman had just been telling her how you killed yourself?' Again the assertion of suicide, again dropped perfectly naturally. Lambert could hardly ask yet if Denise Freeman had sounded like a murderess, which would have been the only real point of his question. It was time to release a little more information.

'Mr and Mrs Robson, what I have to tell you now may distress you. We are fairly certain that Stanley Freeman did not kill himself.' His linguistic instincts rebelled against the imprecision of that 'fairly certain', but it was his professional skills which had chosen the expression. Sooner or later, he would be questioning a murderer: perhaps he was doing so at this moment. He would do everything possible to keep his subjects feeling their way, so that he could observe the process; there was always the chance of a false step.

Here there was none. The Robsons looked at each other in amazement. Between them, Lambert saw their wedding photograph on top of the television set. If they no longer looked the striking couple of a quarter of a century ago, they had nevertheless worn well. Young beauty has an openness and a vulnerability about it. The Robsons now had the poise and watchfulness of experience. It would not be

120

easy to draw from this intelligent and supportive couple anything they did not want to reveal.

Audrey Robson said dully as the news sank in, 'You mean he was murdered.'

George, suitably shocked, said accusingly, 'When you asked me if Denise was upset, you wanted to know whether she sounded like a killer.'

Lambert shrugged away the distasteful necessities of his vocation. 'If you like, but it's a little melodramatic. Once a death becomes a murder inquiry, any reaction is interesting, especially from the next of kin. People in shock are unguarded. If, for example, Mrs Freeman had revealed that she had been half-expecting something of this kind, that would be significant in itself. It might also mean she had some thoughts on who planned this death.'

'It was planned?' said Audrey Robson numbly. Her husband glanced sharply at her.

'Oh yes. This death was not the result of sudden, impulsive violence. It was premeditated, even ingenious.' He was firm and definite, looking for evidence of fear as he firmed up the story. But he told no more than he needed to: they would know the place of the death, but he had revealed neither the time nor the method. He watched the Robsons for any evidence of more knowledge than they should have. He felt his pulse quickening, his senses at their most acute as he confronted the enigma familiar now from so many investigations: was this the perfectly innocent exchange it so far seemed, or an elaborate game of ploy and counter-ploy with a murderer on his guard?

Robson was calm enough to try now a touch of irony. He said, 'Denise seemed shocked but quiet. Remember I only heard her on the phone. I don't know how a murderer should sound.' He had not ruled out the possibility of Denise Freeman as murderer, had indeed brought the question back into focus after his wife's distraction.

Lambert said formally, 'I have to ask you, Mr Robson, as I shall ask everyone close to the deceased, to give me an account of your movements on Wednesday night.'

As Hook flicked to a new page of his notebook, Audrey Robson looked horrified. The reality of a murder inquiry was beginning to bite: a lock of the neat silver hair had somehow escaped and hung down over her left eye, looking quite wild against the exactness of the rest. Her fingers trembled just enough to draw attention to the delicate pink of her nails. When she turned protectively towards her husband, he chose to seem oblivious of the concern he must have remarked in her as he accounted for his movements on the night of the murder.

'That's easy enough. I had a viewing at six-thirty. A Mr and Mrs Swanton—a semi near the centre of Oldford. They would confirm that; I don't have their phone number but we'll have it on file at the office. I got home at about seven-fifteen, I think.' His wife nodded an eager confirmation. Robson had the air of a man being careful about serious matters. 'We ate more or less straight away; Audrey had the meal ready.' As his wife brushed her stray curl distractedly back towards its place, he brought his hands together and contemplated them. They were broad, short-fingered hands. Hands that could easily have restrained the arms of a dying Stanley Freeman: Robson held them up before him with finger-ends steepled together, as if displaying how steady they were at this key point in his story.

John Lambert's wife Christine would have been appalled to see him in action at this moment. For he was enjoying his work, and she knew him well enough to know it, even when he scarcely realized it himself. He prompted his subject with, 'And between eight and nine?' If Robson guessed this was the crucial time, so be it: he would find out soon enough, and he was committed now to the account he had begun. Lambert was quite prepared to stoke the tension and study his reactions.

Robson was smiling. 'You'll need a statement from Fred here.' The labrador, prone at Hook's feet, lifted his head at the sound of his name. 'I was up on the common with him as usual. Always between about eight and nine in the summer. We have to go earlier as the nights close in, of course.' He leaned over towards Hook and fondled the dog's ears, looking down at him indulgently. 'He's a one-man dog, is Fred.'

'I presume Mrs Lambert can confirm the time you left and returned,' said Lambert neutrally. It was the kind of alibi normally confined to the innocent: the guilty often contrived apparently watertight stories. This was more convincing than having spent the evening entirely at home with his wife; spouses' evidence was always suspect, though it could not always be disproved. The diligent police checking which was integral to a murder inquiry would no doubt throw up someone who had conversed with Robson, or at least seen him on the common with the dog.

Hook was dutifully on cue as usual. When he asked, 'Did you speak to anyone up there?' Audrey Robson looked at him as if he had accused her man of lying.

Robson took it calmly enough, as a logical extension of his story. He pursed his lips and thought for a moment, then said, 'Wednesday night. It's difficult, because one night merges with another when you go up there all the time. I can't remember actually speaking to anyone on Wednesday, though I may have done. The regular dog-walkers often have a chat up there: but it was a lovely evening—like

124

tonight. We went right up on to the moor, I think. Wednesday is Audrey's bridge day so Fred had been in for most of the day and was ready for a run. He was chasing rabbits; he never catches any but he enjoys the chase.' Fred sat up and scratched, then put his head on his master's knee and stretched out a large fawn paw, as if he had been offered the highest canine acclaim.

'He was back here about nine,' said Audrey Robson.

'And then here for the rest of the evening. You can examine me on the telly programmes if you like.'

'Except that he probably fell asleep as usual!' said Audrey. Both of them seemed relaxed now, as if they knew they were past the most important time in the evening. George stood up, went across to the alcove by the fireplace, and picked up a handsome decanter.

'Glass of port? Or do you have to say, "Sorry, sir, not on duty"?'

Lambert saw from the elaborate ormolu clock that it was twenty past nine: Robson must have come in at nine o'clock as he said he normally did. He said, 'When we get beyond a twelve-hour day, the rules seem less important. Thank you very much. Sergeant Hook may dutifully refuse, being a puritanical beer drinker.' Audrey Robson eased her elegant frame from the chair and insisted on fetching a can of bitter, as if glad of the release afforded by physical movement.

Hook studied the foaming tankard appreciatively, then solemnly intoned in defence of his choice,

'Malt does more than Milton can
To justify God's ways to man.'

Lambert fought to control the descent of his lower jaw before his Sergeant's urbane smile. He said rather desperately to his suspect-turned-host, 'Lovely decanter.'

'Golfing prize,' said Robson as he returned it to the shelf, and the Superintendent, a struggling golfer himself, tried not to give too much respect to this Hercules who had scaled the cut-glass heights he might never conquer. It was a fine port; he savoured the effects of the wall-lights upon the rich crimson in his glass.

Then he said, 'I have to ask you, Mr Robson, if you can think of anyone who might have had a reason to kill Mr Freeman.'

Audrey Robson looked at her husband in alarm, but George was as calm as he had been throughout. After a few seconds he said, 'I wouldn't describe Stanley as a popular man. Rather the reverse, in fact. That doesn't mean I suspect anyone of killing him.' He sipped his port, watching the sparkling effect of light breaking in myriad facets off the cut glass on to his fingers, as if demonstrating anew how

126

steady those fingers were.

Lambert, wanting suddenly to break that composure, asked bluntly, 'What were your own relationships with the deceased?' Robson seemed unshaken, but his wife gasped, her wide grey eyes shocked at such directness.

'He treated George abominably!' she said, her voice rising with anger at the recollection. She was too involved to notice her husband's admonitory glance. 'He's exploited George for years, and done less and less himself. Old Austin Freeman must have turned in his grave!' Belatedly, she saw her husband's face. Lambert waited, knowing the matter could not be left thus.

George Robson looked down at the dog dozing at his feet and sighed. 'Austin Freeman was Stanley's father and the founder of the firm. I joined in nineteen-sixty. At that time, my public school background seemed to help.'

'George is a Harrovian,' said Audrey Robson. She tried to make it a neutral, explanatory statement, but the pride and wonder of it still seeped in after all these years. When young George Robson had driven into her remote valley in the Dales, he had seemed as exotic to the people there as any sheikh. And he had carried her off just as effectively in his MG. Sergeant Hook, sitting beside this romantic figure with a face of stone, looked into his beer and controlled as best he could the racing emotions of a Barnardo's boy.

'My father had a double DFC and had only just left the RAF when I went to Harrow. Those things counted in the years just after the war,' said Robson. Hook warmed to a man who seemed to be apologizing for his schooling. 'I was in the firm for two years before Stanley arrived, and the elder Mr Freeman was kind about my work.'

'You carried the firm as he got older,' interrupted his wife, resentful of his British understatement.

Robson said, 'All right, Audrey,' with a stillness which did not conceal its authority. Lambert thought her a woman not often silenced, but she did not speak again until her husband had finished.

'Fifteen years ago, Austin took Stanley and me into his office one morning and told us he was leaving the firm between us. I think he had already told his son, because Stanley seemed to accept it readily enough. I was delighted to be rewarded for my work.' For the first time since he had joined them, George Robson looked embarrassed.

There was a lengthy pause. Lambert said, 'Perhaps I should tell you that I shall be seeing Stanley Freeman's solicitor tomorrow. It's standard practice when foul play is suspected.'

Robson smiled ruefully. 'Austin Freeman never made it official. At least, no record of his wishes was ever discovered. He died suddenly of a heart attack a month later without making a new will. The old one had been made years earlier when I was starting work as what we would now call a junior negotiator. It left the family business to Stanley as the only child.'

Audrey Robson chewed her lower lip and kept silent. It was Hook who said, 'And Stanley Freeman didn't honour the gentleman's agreement?'

Robson's voice remained low, but now even his polished delivery could not conceal the bitterness. 'Stanley said he did not regard a verbal agreement as binding. He stuck to the original will. As a sop, he made a will leaving the business to me in the event of his decease, with Denise as a sleeping partner. It hardly seemed relevant, as he was three or four years younger than me and we were both in our thirties. We went on as before, with me on a slightly better salary.'

There was silence for several seconds in the comfortable, conventional room, which seemed a strange setting for this tale of old treacheries. When Fred rolled on to his side and gave the low, satisfied grunt which was the prelude to sleep, it rose unnaturally loud. They had heard only one side of the story: dead men can never defend themselves. But there was certainly enough resentment simmering in the room to motivate a killing.

Into the silence, Lambert dropped an apparently inconsequential question, bringing their thoughts back abruptly to the present. 'What car do you drive, Mr Robson?'

If the man was surprised, he gave no sign of it. He said, 'A red Ford Sierra Ghia. It's in the garage now if you want to see it.' Lambert wondered why he was so anxious to show them what he could not think was important in the inquiry. Unless for some reason he knew it was. Perhaps he was merely anxious to get away from the embarrassment of his personal situation at Freeman Estates.

Lambert said, 'You realize this is now a murder inquiry. The initial suspects are those close to the victim, including yourself.' He ignored Audrey Robson's taut face as he watched her husband's cool nod. 'No one is accused. We proceed by elimination. If we clear Mr Freeman's relations and working associates, we shall move on to a wider, secondary circle of people who had contact with the victim.'

'I hope you have to do that in this case,' said Robson. The smile he attempted was neither wide nor relaxed.

'And I have to hope we find the killer in Mr Freeman's immediate circle.' Lambert spoke evenly, but with an answering smile: these two men understood each other now, whatever the facts he would eventually unearth. 'It gets more difficult as we move outwards. As you probably appreciate, I am asking you if you know of anyone in the firm who could expect to profit from this death.'

'Anyone else, you mean,' said Robson grimly. 'Well, Stanley didn't have many friends, as I said. We carried him in the business most of the time. He was competent enough when he wanted to be, and more than that sometimes, especially when it came to new housing developments. He was quite good on big sales, where people liked to deal with the head of the firm; that's why he was handling Lydon Hall completely on his own. But too often he wasn't around when we needed him. In their different ways, Emily Godson, Simon Hapgood, even Jane Davidson all resented him. He never went out of his way to soothe ruffled feathers, and in small firms grievances sometimes accumulate into hatreds. That doesn't mean I can see any of them killing him.'

Lambert noticed that Robson had excluded no one from suspicion, despite his final disclaimer. He stood up to indicate that the interview was at an end, watched the dog rise and stretch, stroked its head reflectively. Hook, who had watched the technique before, waited for the last key question, which would come when the subjects were off guard, in the belief that the serious business was over.

Lambert had taken a step towards the door before he said, 'What about Denise Freeman?'

Robson glanced at his wife before answering. Was it possible lust lurked beneath

131

this urbane exterior? The dark, lithe Denise Freeman, almost the physical antithesis of Audrey Robson, might arouse lubricious imaginings in many men. If George Robson entertained them, he would do well to conceal them from his unswervingly supportive wife.

'She wasn't close to her husband. That doesn't mean she killed him.'

'Not close?' Lambert was proud of the obtuseness he simulated sometimes as a professional tool.

Robson must have been as conscious as the detectives of his wife's appraisal of his words as he picked them out. 'It didn't seem to me a particularly good marriage over the last few years. They were cool with each other; occasionally they bickered in public. Lately I think they went their own ways.'

That phrase usually meant affairs: there was much to learn yet about the dead Stanley and his very much alive wife.

They were on the front doorstep, preparing to descend the four broad stone steps to the path down the front garden, when Lambert asked, 'This will Stanley Freeman made years ago. Has it ever been replaced?'

Robson made no attempt to dissimulate. He had spoken that afternoon to the firm's solicitors whom he had known for thirty years, and found all he needed to know from a series of embarrassed denials. He looked past them, while scents drifted up from flowers invisible in the late summer darkness, and said, 'Denise will be a sleeping partner, taking a small percentage of profits. Otherwise, Freeman Estates passes to me now.'

His nervous little laugh echoed in their ears all the way down the unlit path.

CHAPTER THIRTEEN

The weather held for the funeral. The dappled shade of the trees round the old churchyard scarcely moved on the bright, still morning. The slow ritual of interment gave Stanley Freeman a dignity he had rarely been afforded in life.

It was Denise Freeman who had decided upon a burial rather than a cremation. They had been married long ago in a Catholic church, and Stanley had been made to promise that the children they had never had would be brought up in that faith. She no longer attended regularly herself, but the influence of those unsmiling French nuns of her childhood, with their faces of ancient parchment, was with her still, long after she had thought it dead. Mumbo-jumbo she might assert it all to be, in the spacious and brilliant drawing-rooms of her friends, but some superstitions were better respected than ignored.

It was cool in the small stone church. She

wished the funeral men would not shuffle their feet as they brought the coffin down the aisle. With its polished brass fittings, its inscribed plate, its single large wreath, the coffin brought its usual moment of breathless silence, as the thought of its contents forced itself upon even the most sluggish of imaginations.

Denise Freeman's imagination was scarcely sluggish. The occasion crystallized the strange, unexpected mixture of emotions she had felt since they had brought to her the news of Stanley's death. There was regret for what might have been, deeper than she had ever thought to feel. There was guilt for attempts left unmade and deceits carefully organized. There was uncertainty about her immediate plans, disconcerting to one used to making decisions and projecting her certainties to those around her. There was elation at her freedom from a marriage which had long ceased to work. But over all, most disturbing because least expected, there was a numbing loneliness about the future which stretched before her, a feeling of solitariness which threatened to descend into panic.

'Out of the depths I have cried to thee, O Lord. Lord, hear my prayer.' The priest intoned the ancient words, happy to retreat from the uneasy platitude of consolation in an age which did not believe. His tiny congregation struggled raggedly to make the half-forgotten responses; only the three elderly women at the back who attended all the services were confident of their words. Denise was glad Stanley's old mother had gone before him: she would have been the only one in the church who felt crippling, undiluted grief.

When they moved outside to the graveyard, there was one other such, but Denise neither saw nor knew her.

The undertaker's men shouldered the coffin with practised ease, moving without a stumble over the uneven paths between the green mounds. Behind them, the widow headed the pathetically diminished procession of mourners. She was the only relative to witness the end of the Freeman line, for Stanley's cousins had declined the long journey from the North. Now George Robson even detached his wife from the group; after their whispered colloquy, Audrey remained in the porch of the church.

So Freeman was followed to his last resting place only by his wife and his employees. The sombre formal garb which was their concession to mourning did not sit easily on all of them, and their modernity was an odd contrast to the priest who accompanied them, in his white alb and purple stole. He swung his stoup of holy water on its chain as the five gathered with him by the grave. And Stanley Freeman's murderer looked with the others into the pit which had been dug to receive his remains.

They stood on the strips of plastic grass which fringed the grave. Denise resented this ersatz turf. It seemed so unnecessary on this dry, bright morning; no doubt it was standard practice. Across the grave she watched the shining black shoes of Simon Hapgood; she had not once looked into his face.

Simon, though, was watching her and wondering what she felt behind her tearless exterior. He was white with the drama of the occasion, filled as he watched the coffin descend with emotions he could not analyse about the man he had cuckolded so cheerfully in life. His light colouring accentuated his paleness; with his smartly cut dark blue suit, his gold-pinned black tie and white cuffs, he could not dismiss the feeling that he must make a wholly appropriate effect at this moment. He wished Denise Freeman would look at him. But he supposed they were playing a scene for watching eyes.

Beside him, Emily Godson, veteran of many funerals, tried not to become preoccupied with the speck of damp clay that had tumbled from the diggings and attached itself obstinately to the black patent leather of her left shoe. She was quiet, controlled, her mien as correct as the charcoal grey of her costume as she watched the ropes lowering the coffin into its last deep cavity. Only a close observer would have seen the strain about her mouth and neck, or the gleam of guilty triumph in her downcast eyes. And none was close enough for that.

The only one watching her was Jane Davidson. Uneasy in the high-heeled shoes she had bought specially for the occasion, standing stiff and straight in the high-necked black dress which might have sat upon her more easily at a cocktail party, she watched the other women for clues as to how she should behave. For at the age of twenty-four it was her first funeral: she had managed to find excuses to miss the two family occasions of her adolescence and now regretted it. She had been anxious lest she should be expected to view the mortal remains of her employer in his coffin, ridiculously grateful that Denise Freeman had afforded such opportunity to no one. She clasped her fingers beneath her folded arms, and when the priest passed the little stoup of holy water around the tiny group, she stepped forward and cast her few drops quickly into the pit, fearful lest the red of her painted nails upon the vessel should be considered an outrageous breach of decorum.

'Ashes to ashes, dust to dust . . .' The priest concluded the valediction with secret relief, and the five cast their earth upon the gleaming plate of the coffin in turn, as if trying already to obliterate the name of Stanley Freeman. George Robson tried to join in with the last prayer, 'Eternal rest grant unto him, O Lord, and let perpetual light shine upon him . . .' but only Denise Freeman's voice rang out clear and knowledgeable with the words to support the priest. George looked across at her, erect, dignified, dark hair sleek and elegant as ever beneath the unaccustomed pillbox hat with its fringe of black net. With her feet placed carefully together on the unnaturally bright green plastic, the slim suppleness of her body seemed only accentuated by the formal garb of mourning. Her voice did not waver, her first tear of the day did not fall until she threw her handful of earth on to the coffin in her last gesture to the spouse that was gone. He tried not to find her sexually attractive at this least appropriate of moments; and failed.

Sergeant Hook, who had married late and had young sons, was disturbed by a different image. He stood with Lambert by the side of the church, sixty yards from the ritual at the graveside. They were in suits of almost identical grey, and they reminded Hook irresistibly of the comic brokers' men in the pantomime he had seen last winter. As the little group moved away from the grave, shaking hands and offering low condolence to the widow, he felt that he and his chief should now move forward and fill the stage with the light relief of knockabout comedy.

They did nothing of the sort, of course. Instead, they continued to observe as losely as possible the behaviour of the funeral's central group. But they learned very little. The murderer might be expected to be reserved, even withdrawn, at the interment of the victim. But here no one was at ease; each participant was careful in behaviour, almost silent. Of this group, only Denise Freeman and George Robson had been at the inquest, where Lambert had had a more active role.

The widow had been as contained there as she was now, giving her evidence of identification with no sign of physical distress, receiving the Coroner's sympathy with no more than a nod and the slightest of smiles, whether of gratitude or irony it was impossible to tell. She had remained calm even through the pathologist's evidence. His account of the marks of physical restraint upon the corpse's wrists, his seeming regret at the absence of any alien skin tissue beneath the nails, had brought no shudders of distress from Mrs Freeman. She had heard the finding of 'Murder by person or persons unknown' without any sign of emotion, had left the court without the assistance of George Robson's proffered arm.

The two large men stood well to one side amid the old gravestones as Audrey Robson rejoined her husband and clasped his hand. The party moved off to their various cars. Lambert wished he could observe the inevitable unbending at the small reception which would follow at the Freemans' bungalow, but there were some doors closed even to senior policemen investigating murder.

He watched the Robsons, now in animated conversation in their car. He was so occupied with conjecture that he scarcely registered the footsteps on the gravel behind him.

'You're in charge of this case, aren't you, sir?' The last word, a diffident addition, told him before he turned that this was one not at ease with the police. She must in her youth have been buxom; now age and callous accuracy might more readily suggest blowsy. The yellow hair did not look natural, though the blue straw hat perched ridiculously upon it concealed the roots. She had done her best to dress for a funeral, but the tights that had looked navy in the dimness of her room were almost royal blue in the sun's strong light, the trimmings of the grey dress insistently yellow, the heels of the black shoes worn low beneath their inappropriate straps. The features must have been pretty in youth; their present coarseness had been accentuated by crying, so that the wrinkles round the puffy eyes were stressed rather than disguised by powder. Lambert felt a sudden, overwhelming tenderness as he divined why she was here. But it was Bert Hook who said, 'Come into the church, love, and sit down. It's quiet there now.'

She walked meekly between them. Lambert knew where he had seen her before. She had sat in the public gallery at the inquest, looking strained and shocked at the evidence. While those around her had been filled with excitement, she had rolled and unrolled a man's damp handkerchief between her too-active fingers. Now, as if to activate Lambert's memory, she delved into a grey plastic handbag and produced another, smaller handkerchief to dab at her eyes.

They sat at the back of the dim, deserted church and Hook said quietly, 'What did you want to tell us?' He could be perceptive as well as direct: most sergeants would have taken her name and other details first.

'It may be nothing.' Her determination was draining now that she was actually with the police.

'Never mind, tell us.'

'It's just that Stanley—Mr Freeman—was with me on the night he died. I didn't tell the police in Gloucester properly. I was—confused.' The word conjured up for all of them an uncomfortable picture of her interview.

'What time did he meet you?' asked Lambert.

'He came to my flat at about seven as usual.'

'This was a regular arrangement?' said Bert Hook gently. Lambert, recognizing his expertise, let him ask the rest of the questions.

'Yes. For two years now.' She could not keep a little pride out of her voice. Then, as the wrongness of the 'now' struck her, the first sob shook the curves that were just too ample.

'When did he leave you?'

'It must have been about eight. He had an appointment at eight-thirty, an important one that he couldn't break. But he was coming back afterwards.' Even on this summer morning the back of the church seemed cool and damp, as they pictured this pitiable creature waiting alone into the night for a lover who would never return.

They took the routine details from her then: the length of the affair, the frequency of their meetings, the people who knew about it. She had thought there were none: yet someone had told the uniform branch at Gloucester about Stanley's visits. She had not thought how a new Granada would excite attention and jealousy in the streets where she lived. She was glad they did not ask her about Stanley's regular monthly payments to her. Eventually, she even ventured a little about their plans for the future, and they were careful to show no scepticism about the dead man's intentions.

Margot Jomes had made the awkward journey by bus, and Hook on a nod from his chief offered her a lift home, but she refused. She came out of the church with them, seeming hardly to notice the transition to a brightness which made them blink. They left her standing alone in the deserted churchyard, a silhouette who might have stepped straight from Hardy.

She was the only unequivocal weeper in this last chapter of Stanley Freeman's existence.

CHAPTER FOURTEEN

It was less than three miles from the churchyard to Lydon Hall, but Lambert drove the big Vauxhall slowly, reflecting upon the images of the funeral.

'What news on the suicide note?' he asked Hook eventually.

'Nothing very useful. It was typed on one of the machines at Freeman Estates: electronic, but our people are certain enough to swear to it in court. It's actually the one Emily Godson uses most frequently, but any of them had easy access to it. Including Freeman himself, of course.'

'What about Denise Freeman?'

'She has a key to the office. She could have got in any time when it was quiet. The note could have been prepared weeks ago, of course.'

'And the signature?'

'Genuine Stanley Freeman, in the view of the calligraphy boys. As he habitually signed letters without reading them, and on occasions blank sheets of paper waiting for messages to be typed above his name, it wouldn't have been difficult to obtain.'

Lambert frowned what was no more than a standard reaction. He had never expected this murderer to help them in so obvious a way.

But it was another path of investigation that had turned into a blind alley. Perhaps through some superstition that he would close another path in this way, he was quite reluctant as he said, 'Any news on the car the Harbens saw near Lydon Hall?'

'No other sightings of it as yet.'

That probably indicated it was local. If a car had been driven across the county in that reckless manner, the police would probably have turned up some other person who had noticed it by now. As he parked at the old Hall, Lambert said, 'What about our suspects' cars?'

'The only one who has a blue one is Simon Hapgood. As you know, the Harbens weren't sure of make or model. Rushton has shown them the manufacturers' publicity pictures of Hapgood's car in blue, but they couldn't be certain. They'd be no use against a defence counsel, of course.'

'No.' He made a mental note to investigate the matter with young Mr Hapgood, though. He had watched him with interest at the funeral.

They walked past the impressive elevations of the old house, looked automatically at the French windows and the spot where Freeman's body had been discovered. The gardens were trim, the stone terrace mellow in the sun. There was nothing sinister here; the house, which had seen older and darker tragedies,

144

had swallowed this small death effortlessly into its history. In the arboretum, they moved among squirrels and birds who had grown used now to being undisturbed here. They sensed before they entered the sturdy wooden summerhouse that it was empty. Wino Willy was more of this world than theirs: they would scarcely catch him unawares. There was no glimpse of nervous eyes behind the dusty window, no sign this time of the swift, erratic, scarcely human movement of his flight.

Nor was there evidence of a recent presence within the building. The belongings of this strange squatter were precious few, but he had removed them. The cane table had lost its mug and spoon and the ragged blanket was gone from the seat by the door. 'No condensed milk,' said Lambert, recalling with a smile the smell from his youth.

'No bread, no packets of soup,' said Hook, ticking off the evidence in a mind trained to observation over the years. 'He'll be up on the moor in this warm weather.'

Lambert nodded: perhaps both of them chose not to confront the idea that they had driven Willy from this dry, warm haven. They followed the narrow track worn through the long grass by their quarry's feet, climbed the fence at the gap in the barbed wire, and set off across the common.

'Are we getting nearer?' said Hook after they had walked a little way. With the advantage of their long acquaintance, both knew he was talking about the murder.

'Not a lot. We're dealing with a cool customer who plans ahead and keeps his nerve.'

'Not hers?' said Hook, almost eagerly: he was old-fashioned enough to find murder more unnatural in females.

'His or hers, Bert. Statistically, it's six to four on a woman in our five.'

'You're still convinced it's one of those five?'

'Convinced is a bit strong. But yes, I think so.' The routine checking of the elaborate police machine that went into action after a murder had not thrown up other possibilities in what was now almost a week. No strangers in the district, no previously undiscovered relatives or acquaintances, no violence elsewhere in the area that might connect with the quietly achieved death at the Hall. 'What did DI Rushton think of the three we haven't interviewed yet?'

Although Lambert and Hook had so far interviewed only two of them, all five of the mourners round the grave had now been seen by the police. Lambert would check his impressions and Hook's notes against their statements in due course, looking for the inconsistencies that might indicate concealment, even guilt. Those who committed this darkest of crimes took on a

146

large organization, developed by experience and technology to a high proficiency. Just occasionally, if they were cool and clever and lucky—it usually required all three qualities—they were successful.

Bert Hook, who had read through Inspector Rushton's report as directed while Lambert was in conference with the Chief Constable that morning, considered how best to summarize his findings. Rushton, keen and a little officious, was ten years his junior, but Hook had no envy of his superior rank.

'He didn't like Mr Hapgood. But he doesn't think he did it. He quite liked young Jane Davidson, and he doesn't think she did it. Emily Godson didn't like him, doesn't seem to have much of an alibi, and he hopes she did it.' Rushton would have been aghast at this unprofessional summary of hours of interviews; Hook thought it rather succinct.

They were climbing now, winding slowly over the common as the small town of Oldford opened like a relief map on their left. Already the graveyard they had recently left looked far distant on the other edge of the settlement, though it could have been scarcely more than two miles away in a direct line. Hook, narrowing keen eyes against the sun, thought the earth was already being restored over the coffin of Stanley Freeman, but it might have been no more than fancy: he was too far away to distinguish movement. On the nearer side of the town, the Robsons' square, solid house was just coming into view above the trees as they climbed higher. Hook could see the back door and kitchen window quite clearly, but there was no sign of the amiable and enthusiastic Fred.

'Could Emily Godson have done it?' It was the first time Lambert had spoken for a good five minutes.

'Not if she was where she says she was,' said Hook. 'She says she was with a client of the firm throughout the period between eight and nine.'

'That should be easy enough to confirm,' said Lambert, cheerful at the prospect of a straightforward elimination of at least one of his subjects.

'DI Rushton thought there was something phoney about Simon Hapgood, but he couldn't catch him out,' said Hook. Lambert wondered if it might be no more than a clash of temperaments. Hapgood, with his slightly epicene good looks and smart clothes, had looked like a youngish man on the make. Rushton was in some respects rather similar, though he would have been appalled to know that Lambert had recognized the qualities. He was doing well enough himself, but, hemmed in by the boundaries of police procedures, he probably envied Hapgood's greater scope in a rising property market. Speculation. Rushton was a diligent, industrious detective: if he

148

thought all was not as it seemed here, his superintendent would do well to heed his opinion.

'Why doesn't he fancy the flair Miss Davidson?' said Lambert, regretting his phrasing even before it was complete.

'I'm sure he does!' said Hook, relishing this rare lapse, 'but as a murderer, she seems to have had neither opportunity nor motive.'

'Opportunity I like. If we can prove she wasn't in the area, fine. Motive we may simply not have discovered so far.' Lambert, remembering Jane Davidson's composure at the graveside, would have preferred to see more grief. Despite her pallor, her air had been one of indifference, even satisfaction, which seemed somehow the more shocking because of her relative youth. Perhaps it was no more than a front, a show of bravado lest her emotional turmoil be exposed. The young could be tiresome at times. But he remembered what the other woman suspect, Denise Freeman, had said about the dead man and Jane: 'I doubt whether he was bedding her, though it never pays to underestimate the naïvety of the young. But she seemed to have some hold over him.' He wondered with a grim smile what Jane might think of the astute and enigmatic widow.

They moved off the common now, on to the wilder moorland beyond, climbing steadily through heather and patches of bracken towards the long line where earth met sky. They must have been several hundred feet high when they approached a disused sheepfold, its four dry-stone walls forming a ragged square. It was well away from any path, in a small hollow beside a tiny brawling stream. Hook had known where to look, or they would have passed without discovering the place. At its furthest corner, where the prevailing west wind would sweep wildly over its stones on stormy nights, three rusting corrugated iron sheets formed a rough roof, providing a shelter within which was perhaps twelve feet square. From the shadowy interior of this improvised lair, their quarry watched them with the quick, mobile eyes of an animal used to flight and evasion. With the sudden, piercing insight of a mind which had slipped off balance, he knew why they had come.

They moved in cautiously after he had seen them, a little surprised that he did not flee from them as he had once before. But then he had been a trespasser: here he was on his own ground. The distinction was perfectly clear in Willy's damaged mind.

They took in the empty bottles, the two battered biscuit tins, the plastic dish on the ground which had once held food but which now held a little water. Lambert realized that some wild animal, perhaps more than one, had been here within touching distance of Willy.

There were four wine bottles, all empty. He

150

did not smell of drink; perhaps in a more confined space he would have done. They looked from the bottles to the man, and his eyes followed theirs. 'Well then, Willy,' said Bert Hook quietly.

Wino Willy looked at the bottles, then allowed a small, secret smile to come upon him. He rocked back and forth on his haunches, glanced up at the sky, and said, '"Poor Tom's a-cold."' Shakespeare knew all about the wisdom of fools and madmen: Willy felt himself in good hands. He folded his arms and drew his imaginary rags about him.

He had in fact a thick coat about his shoulders, too warm if anything for this summer's day. Lambert, struggling to follow the working of this twisted, agile mind, wondered how to proceed.

'I was sorry to hear about your boy,' he said desperately. He meant it: who wouldn't be sorry who had heard the sad tale of Wino Willy Harrison? But he had not known that son, and the words rang false to himself even as he said them, a means to an end, a cheap way past a sick man's defences.

Willy flashed him a momentary look of outrage, plucked an imaginary sprig of vegetation from the air in front of him, flicked it contemptuously towards his tormentor's face, and cried, 'There's rosemary. That's for remembrance!'

'Sorry,' said Lambert. Even Hook, who had

151

little idea what was going on, caught Willy's bitterness.

'We're here about a death,' said Lambert, contriving to sound to himself both trite and desperate.

'"The Angel of Death hath spread his wings,"' intoned Willy. He leapt upright and opened his arms above them like some Victorian tombstone sculpture.

'"Any man's death diminishes me,"' said Lambert without thinking. And evoked at least a quick glance of sympathy amid the mockery.

'"To every man upon this earth
Death cometh soon or late,"'

said Willy.

'"Death lays its icy hand on kings,"' said Lambert. He was desperate to keep the contact going, but had no idea where this ridiculous game of quotations could lead; he tried not to look at Hook.

Perhaps the bard purged Willy's contempt and brought him back to his own strange and tragic reality. He said quietly,

'"Golden lads and girls all must,
As chimney-sweepers, come to dust,"'

and Lambert, catching his mood correctly this time, picked up the familiar words

152

of consolation,

> ' "Fear no more the heat of the sun,
> Nor the furious winter's rages." '

Hook, sitting on a flat stone and studying the cold ashes of a dead fire, could scarcely believe his ears as he heard the two voices above him in quiet union on the next lines,

> ' "Thou thy worldly task hath done,
> Home art gone and ta'en thy wages." '

There was a long silence, perhaps a full minute, as Willy thought of his lost son, Lambert regretted the crudity of his original attempt to use that memory, and Hook wished he were miles from here.

Then Lambert said reluctantly, 'Our death was a murder, Willy.' The words hung heavy in this lonely place. Hook thought that injured brain had not registered the distinction between death and murder, but Lambert had seen the brown eyes flash briefly within their dark hollows. The quick mind had its quotation ready. Willy said gruffly,

> ' "Truth will come to light; murder cannot be hid long." '

Lambert said, 'Yes, Willy, but we need your help to bring this truth to light. We think you

153

might have seen something.'

> ' "The little dog laughed
> To see such sport,
> And the dish ran away with the spoon." '

Willy was away across the sheepfold like a wild thing. Lambert thought he had finally lost the thread of connection with that strange mind, until they saw the object of his attention. A black and white mongrel dog stood on its hind legs, its front paws on the lowest part of the wall, its head on one side. Willy was with it in a second, his two hands stretched to fondle its ears.

> ' "Young blood must have its course, lad,
> And every dog its day," '

called Willy. Then he vaulted the uneven stone wall and leapt away like a schoolboy with his delighted canine friend.

' "Thou shalt do no murder," ' called Lambert desperately, reduced to the Book of Common Prayer as he saw his witness disappearing.

Willy stopped dead and turned back towards them. He enjoyed this quotation game, the first stretching of his brain for pure amusement that he had known in several years. He called across bracken and heather to his partner in this intellectual conspiracy.

' "For murder, though it have no tongue, will speak
With most miraculous organ." '

Then he turned and flung a stick for his new companion, wild and high into the bracken, cackling delightedly as the dog leapt high over ferns in pursuit.

Lambert turned back to a perplexed Hook. 'That was young Hamlet's view of things,' he said in explanation. When his sergeant looked disapproving, he added triumphantly, 'He said it just before he staged the first recorded reconstruction of a violent crime. Forward-looking as always, the moody Dane.'

They saw Wino Willy once more. As they began their descent from the moor, they glimpsed him above them, sitting with the dog between his feet on a knoll of ground, perhaps two hundred yards away. The birds wheeled around the motionless pair, some of them settling even as they watched. They took bread from his fingers, so that even as the police-men watched, Wino Willy was transformed to a latter-day Francis of Assisi.

They thought he had not seen them, but in this world Willy was as alert as a wild thing to his surroundings. As they turned to depart, he called to them through the clear, sun-warmed air, startling the larks above and the stonechats below. " 'The more I see of men, the better I like dogs." '

His valediction rang in their ears as they trod carefully back towards the world of men. Hook was disappointed but phlegmatic about what seemed another dead end. He had enjoyed the walk, and he had not expected much from Wino Willy anyway. What he could not understand was the elation which his chief was striving so ineffectively to conceal. The ways of superintendents were arcane indeed, but surely the intellectual contest alone could not have so excited him?

Lambert, wrestling with his recall of that contest, was certain there were clues to the mystery within it somewhere. He had not managed to isolate them yet. But in due course he would return to the strange world of Wino Willy.

CHAPTER FIFTEEN

The offices of Arkwright and Sons were touched with the genteel shabbiness which indicates long standing and reliability in the legal profession. The Georgian windows were dusty but genuine; the front door with its polished brass fittings had the myriad small scratches of age, but it was solid mahogany. Inside the building, the doors were low and the rooms small, but little altered since the days when clerks on high stools copied documents in copperplate. This place said, 'We were here a century and more ago, and we shall be here a century hence. Put your trust in us.'

Alfred Arkwright could hardly have provided a greater contrast with Wino Willy. He was probably ten years older: Lambert's first thought was that he would comfortably outlive that broken being. The solicitor's silver hair was impeccably groomed, the skin on his perfectly shaved face gleamed on the high cheekbones. The blue eyes telegraphed interest, but polite, discreet interest. The small hands with their spotless nails would protect you against the petty ploys of the unscrupulous. The gold-rimmed spectacles seemed not merely an aid to better sight but an accessory added to guarantee the competence of this guardian of respectability.

They sat in leather armchairs while he poured the coffee: it would never have done to have had a third party overhear their discussion. His suit was probably fifteen years old; even Hook noticed the narrow, perfectly pressed lapels. It was nowhere threadbare: probably it was one of many in Arkwright's wardrobe. Like the building, the furnishings, the man himself, it exuded quiet, established quality. In this place, ostentation might be the worst of sins, but everything was ordered, unchanging, reassuring. Wino Willy Harrison's landscape of wide skies and singing, wind-tossed birds was a different world indeed.

Alfred Arkwright used deliberation as a professional tool. Lambert was in a hurry to complete this routine business, but there was no way he could alter the solicitor's measured pace. Carefully, he checked the detail of George Robson's account of wills and intentions. 'Austin Freeman was a highly respected figure in the town,' said Arkwright with fond reminiscence. The implication of what followed was that his son Stanley was altogether less reliable. Yes, Austin had clearly indicated his intention of leaving the business jointly to his son Stanley and George Robson. But he had never made a will to that effect; Arkwright's shrug acknowledged yet another example of human frailty undermining the best legal advice.

Stanley Freeman had apparently chosen to ignore his father's clearly expressed intention. Alfred Arkwright's look of distaste was not for the morality of the action but for the laxity of legal provision that allowed it. He showed just the right amount of reluctance to divulge the details of the will of Stanley himself: he was experienced enough to know that a murder inquiry made this essential, but decorum demanded a little well-bred resentment of this invasion of his territory.

Lambert, his mood still preoccupied with thoughts of the injured mind they had left on the moor, eventually became impatient with this effete and civilized ritual. 'Mr Arkwright, both you and I know that you're going to tell us everything eventually. I'd prefer that we didn't have to wring it from you by means of a long list of questions and answers to satisfy your imagined scruples. Please tell us straightforwardly exactly what Mrs Denise Freeman is left in the will.'

Alfred Arkwright had for a moment the sullen face of a frustrated schoolboy. Lambert had spoken brusquely, probably because his mind was still dominated by the image of Willy Harrison silhouetted against the sky with dog and birds. The solicitor recovered his equilibrium quickly; losing face was the ultimate crime for him, and any ruffling of his urbanity must be taken as a warning. 'She gets the bungalow, Glebe House, which was the family home, her car, various shareholdings, which will be valued for probate at around £30,000. There are insurance policies which I understand should give her another £50,000.' Arkwright had proposed to dispense this catalogue as a series of gobbets of information; it was a habit, no more.

'And the business?' said Lambert.

'Mrs Freeman will be entitled to five per cent of the profits per year for the rest of her life.' If Arkwright thought the arrangement unusual, he gave no sign of it in his demeanour.

'What about control of the firm?'

'That passes entirely to Mr Robson, together with the ownership of the company.'

'Conscience money,' said Bert Hook, speaking for the first time, without looking up from his notes. Arkwright's small smile might have been a grudging acknowledgement, might have been a contemptuous dismissal of an idea so squalid and emotional. He put his coffee cup and saucer carefully back on the tray. Speculation was certainly no part of his brief.

For the men before him, speculation was inevitable. George Robson had already indicated that he knew the terms of Freeman's will and the motive it gave him. No doubt Denise Freeman knew also. Resentment could turn to hatred when nursed in holy wedlock. Many a husband had been killed by an embittered spouse. Lambert wondered how much Denise knew about Margot Jones.

He was reluctant to add the question he knew he must. 'Were there any other financial bequests?'

'None. There are no family retainers in the Freeman household.' Arkwright examined his perfectly manicured nails. His ordered and respectable world did not admit mistresses, though wills sometimes contained puzzling and suggestive clauses. Poor Margot, thought Lambert. The only person who genuinely grieved for Stanley Freeman, perhaps the only one who really needed material provision, was ignored in the will. Stanley's death had shut her out of his world more finally than the thickest of doors.

The detectives were standing now, ready to go. Perhaps it was their haste that ruffled Arkwright into volunteering information for the first time. He said, 'There is one provision which strikes me as rather strange.' His pained expression regretted that he should be beset by any such controversial opinion. 'Not exactly financial, but I think we could say with financial implications.' The cautious verbosity reassured him and his tone resumed its former suavity. He reached into the file in front of him, but they all knew he had the detail clear in his mind without such check. 'It concerns the ownership of a bungalow. No. 3, Acacia Avenue, Oldford. It is occupied at present, I understand, by an elderly lady, who lives there rent-free. A Miss Alice Franklyn.'

'Who owns it?' said Lambert shortly. He had tired again of massaging this carefully assumed panache.

'It *was* owned by Stanley Freeman. The clause I referred to says that on his decease it should pass to someone else. Not the occupier.'

Lambert was now thoroughly impatient with this absurd ritual of small delays. 'Who?' he said harshly.

'Miss Emily Godson,' said the solicitor.

161

CHAPTER SIXTEEN

They thought at first that there was no one in the house. Hook rang the bell twice, but there was no sound of answering movement within. Maple Cottage was a comfortable, low-slung building. Its low front wall and wicket gate made one expect a cottage garden, with old-fashioned perennials growing into each other and the scent of honeysuckle overriding more subtle and individual ones.

Probably the garden had originally been like that. And no doubt in those days its fertility had been abundantly supplemented by the products of an outside privy: Bert Hook, who was a modest expert in this field, would willingly have enlarged on what was now denied to a hungry soil. Some time after this radical change in sanitation, the garden had been changed to a more formal pattern. A small, immaculately manicured lawn followed the curve of the path towards the front door. Neat rows of lobelia, tagetes and antirrhinums were already in lusty flower and would soon merge into variegated carpets around the cerise and red geraniums that were dotted among them as specimen plants. It should have been like park bedding, but, perhaps because of the low walls that surrounded it and the absence of straight lines, it remained

162

curiously intimate amid its seed-packet profusion of colour. On the tiny porch which enclosed the front door, a climbing rose dangled its scented, crimson blooms and maintained the memory of the cottage's older history. Skilfully photographed, it could still adorn the lid of one of those chocolate boxes which take the evocation of a former age as the only guarantee of quality.

Lambert toyed with this thought, studying the angle a photographer would choose. As he looked towards the corner of the cottage, a figure materialized silently at this very point. In silhouette against the light, she might for a second have been part of his fancied Victorian picture. Her neat white blouse had enough lace to be in period, even if its material was manmade and its decorations machined. But the tweed skirt showed sturdy ankles and calves which would have scandalized Victorian mores.

'You're early.' Emily Godson made it sound like an accusation. Hook was glad he had not been caught peering through the windows into an empty house.

'A little, I'm afraid, Miss Godson.' Lambert was at his most affable. 'We had to change our plans and come to see you before Mr Hapgood. I did try to phone you earlier.' He didn't tell her that it had been Alfred Arkwright's one unexpected piece of information that had steered them hither

163

so directly.

'I've been in the greenhouse. I thought I might as well take advantage of the leisure you compelled upon me.'

Why couldn't the wretched woman accept graciously the windfall bonus of time spent in the garden she so obviously loved? 'I thought you'd find our interview less embarrassing here than at the station.' Lambert could threaten if he had to. Then he said, 'You've got your garden looking quite beautiful.' The three of them looked round, while Hook murmured sycophantic support.

'You'd better come inside,' said Emily Godson gruffly, mollified despite her worst intentions. Lambert accepted tea, to Hook's scarcely muted delight, and presently they sat in a low-ceilinged parlour, balancing Crown Derby saucers with infinite care upon their ample laps.

'My mother's. She died four years ago,' said Miss Godson. Lambert wished the Alfred Arkwrights of this world could be made to dispense information so quickly.

'She lived here with you?' It was not just small talk. He wanted to build up as full a picture as he could of his suspects, and he had learned little of Emily Godson from his colleagues' preliminary reports. 'She had her children here, nursed my father through his last illness here, died here herself,' said Emily. It would have sounded sentimental with a

164

different delivery, but this woman was brisk and matter-of-fact. She would find it easier to conceal than to reveal emotion, even when it was that most laudable love of a daughter who had missed marriage to care for a widowed mother. If marriage was indeed the boon that idea demanded. They looked down the narrow back garden to where the maple which gave the house its name was a mound of amber in the sun. That was where the privy must have been, thought Hook; what a pity not to have a patch of brassicas taking full advantage of its opulent legacy.

'You have brothers and sisters?' said Lambert quietly. He was looking at the greenhouse at the other corner of the garden's extremity. How on earth did anyone manage to keep such a place so tidy? There was not a pot or a box visible between its aluminium glazing bars save those which contained plants; what a contrast to his own large and disorderly glasshouse, where bags of compost mingled with sprays, crocks and discarded grow-bags amid the tomatoes.

'I have a brother, that's all,' said the woman on his left. Something in her tone transferred his attention from the garden to her face. It was in its way an impressive face, of the kind an artist would carve rather than paint: it would need a Rembrandt to capture its suggestion of dignified suffering.

'I hadn't heard of a brother,' said Lambert.

165

He felt a small spurt of guilt at this deliberate inference that he already knew a lot about her when in fact they knew so little. Her brown eyes gazed down the garden. Her strong nose looked very straight in profile. The dark, greying hair was cut short and neat, almost masculine around the strong head. From this angle, the determined chin, the high, clean profile, the unexpectedly long lashes showed the striking beauty she must once have been. The large mouth drooped a little at the corners, so that he willed her to the smile he knew would light up her face. Suddenly he understood, more clearly than if she had complained to him for an hour, that this woman had not had very much pleasure from life. There coursed through him one of the sudden, violent surges of sympathy he thought he had left in his childhood, so that he wanted to reach out and touch her.

He did not do it of course. Heaven knows what the world would do if its Superintendents began to behave in that manner. And, as he sat and coldly reminded himself that this might well be a murderess, she did indeed smile. Not quite the smile he had wanted to restore the face's lost beauty. It was too rueful for that: not far from Wino Willy's bitter smile when he had mocked him with rosemary for remembrance.

'Michael doesn't live here any more,' she said. Then she briefly shook her head; perhaps

166

to her as to him it sounded like the title of a play. 'He went to New Zealand ten years and more ago.' It was very quiet now. Outside, a robin hopped along one of the neat lines of plants in search of food. None of the three spoke; all of them sensed the woman was about to make some revelation about herself.

'Mother left him this cottage,' she said. She glanced at them almost apologetically, as if she should have produced something more dramatic. 'Mike is divorced. He needs the money from this place to make a settlement with his wife and keep his farm in New Zealand. Very soon now. He's relying on me to tell him when the market's right to sell this cottage.' She forced a bitter-sweet smile at the memory of it. She had been born here, had grown here to womanhood, had cherished this cottage and garden for the best part of five decades. That unexpected riot of colour in the weed-free garden, this sensibly modernized interior, were her doing; they contained something of her, perhaps more than she cared to admit.

It was Bert Hook, who had not owned a home of his own for the first thirty-six years of his life, who was most aware of the emotion under these quiet statements. 'Why?' he said indignantly. 'Why would your mother do that?' He ignored John Lambert's admonitory glance, telling him he was moving into areas which should be beyond their concern. And as had happened before when staid Bert Hook acted instinctively, there were unexpected dividends. Emily Godson, leaping to the defence of her dead mother, revealed in the next few minutes what might have taken days of inquiry.

'Mother never thought I'd have to move. Mike was doing well and was apparently happily married. The idea was that I'd live here for life—or as long as I wanted to. She thought Mike might eventually want to come back here. I think she hoped he would. Anyway, she thought she'd left me quite secure financially. She left me what little money she had and also—' She stopped, aghast at where she had been led in defence of the mother who was still so definitely with her in this house.

'Also . . . ?' said Hook gently. Emily Godson picked a small piece of dried grass off her skirt, tugged the left sleeve of her blue woollen cardigan a centimetre lower on her wrist, and acknowledged that she could not stop now.

'There was another property, where my aunt lives—my mother's elder sister. Mum left that to her, with the clear understanding that it would come to me at her death.'

'Understanding?' It was the first time Lambert had spoken for five minutes. He had never expected to sound like Alfred Arkwright. Emily looked at him caustically; these were questions she had asked herself *ad nauseam* over the last few months.

168

'Mother didn't understand the law and its necessities. Why should she? Dad used to handle all that sort of thing. And Aunt Alice knew all about it and understood. She was my favourite aunt.' Suddenly this formidable professional woman was near to tears. At this moment, a spotless brown and white cat strolled down the flagged path in the rear garden, elegant, leisurely, too dignified for the petty human concerns within the house. All three of them were glad to observe its progress and wait for Emily to regain control.

'She still *is* my favourite aunt,' said Emily, as if shocked at the disloyalty in her use of the past tense. 'It's just that Mother knew nothing about the problems of senile dementia. And still less about the people around who might take advantage of it.'

'We are talking about 3, Acacia Avenue, I think,' said Lambert quietly. He had seen where this was leading for some time. He told himself his excitement could not be as unworthy as it felt. They were about to find out more about both the dead man and one of his suspects: this thrill of anticipation was a necessary adjunct of efficient detection.

Emily was not offended, as he had half-expected. She seemed no more than mildly surprised that he knew. 'It's a modern detached bungalow,' she said, falling automatically into the jargon of her profession. 'More valuable than this. Mum thought she

169

was looking after me carefully. If Aunt Alice hadn't—' Abruptly, she was weeping as the suffering and anxiety she had hugged to herself for months fell out. Again Lambert had to resist the impulse to touch her, to put the arm round the shoulders that such moments seemed to need. The proprieties of objective investigation must be preserved. He suddenly realized the unbending Miss Godson was longing to throw herself weeping on the breast of the mother she had lost. Hook gathered the crockery carefully together on the tray; any activity was better than this embarrassing detachment.

When Emily resumed, she dropped her sentences in a flat monotone which only emphasized how brittle was the control she had won back. 'Aunt Alice isn't really fit to be on her own any longer, but she doesn't want to move. A home help goes in each morning and I go round every evening. I was there on the Wednesday night that Freeman was killed.'

Automatically, Lambert clocked up the questions. How accurately did she know the time of the death? How much was the word of a senile relative worth in the establishment of an alibi?

If Emily knew she had forestalled questions for the moment by pressing on with her account, she gave no sign of it, for she spoke almost like one under hypnosis. 'We never know quite what we'll find when we go into the bungalow.' There came an unexpected flashing smile at some recollection of humour amid the tragedy, but she did not enlighten them about the incident. 'She's quite harmless, childlike and rather sweet. And not responsible for her actions. Three months ago, she signed the bungalow away to someone else. He'd been round to see her with flowers and cakes. Just three times. It's often those closest who suffer as the mind begins to go, you know.' She offered the last observation as if recounting a detached case history, but the tears sprang anew.

'That person was Stanley Freeman?' said Lambert. It seemed cruel to wring every detail from her distress, when Arkwright had already given them the clue.

She nodded, not shocked that he should know. 'Stanley had heard about her from me. He offered to ease the burden for me by going to sit with her occasionally in the evenings. That was when she signed the bungalow away. It wasn't Aunt Alice's fault. Ten years ago she'd have seen through him straight away and sent him packing.' She was as anxious to defend her aunt as she had been her mother a few minutes earlier. 'It's age that does it,' she said bleakly, as the tears coursed down her cheeks and dropped unheeded on to her white blouse. For a moment she contemplated that most inexorable of enemies, lying in patient wait for her.

'I think you should contact Arkwright and Sons in Oldford,' said Lambert. 'You may find some good news about 3, Acacia Avenue.'

She was so little cheered by the news that he felt cheated. Then he realized that she was exhausted. This parade of emotions by one who had practised containment and self-sufficiency for years had drained her more than it would have done others.

'He said he'd arranged things so that I would get the place back if he died before me,' she said, so quietly that they had to strain to catch her words even in that low, silent room. 'I didn't believe him.' She acknowledged with a sombre smile the knowledge that in this at least she had misjudged him.

Lambert wondered whether he believed her. It was Hook who said after a pause, 'What car do you drive, Miss Godson?'

She looked at him like one who did not see the point of the question. 'A brown Ford Escort, usually.'

'Usually?'

'Well, almost invariably. Freeman always insisted they were pool cars; there are duplicate keys in the office. There are tax advantages, apparently. I always thought it was one of his ways of reminding us who was boss.'

Lambert said, 'Think carefully before you answer this, Miss Godson. Do you know of anyone who would have wished to kill Stanley Freeman?'

172

There were no histrionics. She did as she was bid and considered her reply carefully; for so long that he prompted her with, 'I shall ask others the same question in relation to you.'

She smiled that small, cramped smile that he would so like to have seen enlarged. Then she said, 'There is no one I can see as a murderer. None of us liked him. Sometimes I thought that his wife hated him, at others that she merely despised him. George Robson is highly competent and highly frustrated in his work: I presume that can be an explosive mixture. I don't like Mr Hapgood and I wouldn't trust him, even with the petty cash, but I don't see him as a murderer.'

There was a silence while all three of them weighed what she had said. They all knew there was one name she had not mentioned. She looked up into Lambert's face to check that he was still waiting, then put the tea she had not touched carefully back on the table. Eventually she said, 'There was something between Jane Davidson and Freeman that I didn't understand. I think he had some hold over her —or she over him. But I don't profess to understand the young.' Her face resumed its lines of disapproval at the thought, as if she was preparing to raise again the barriers she had lowered for a time.

Denise Freeman had said something similar about the receptionist at Freeman Estates: Lambert filed away this second suggestion of

173

mystery. For the rest, Emily Godson's assessments might almost have come from one of his subordinates in a dispassionate summary of their suspects. For a moment, he was filled with respect as well as sympathy for the sturdy spirit beneath this spinsterish exterior.

Then, her calmness making the import of the words more shocking, Emily said, 'I'm glad he's dead. I could have killed him myself.'

Bert Hook twitched his surprise, despite his experience. Even hardened detective-sergeants can be caught off guard in that eerie moment when someone voices their very thoughts.

CHAPTER SEVENTEEN

Acacia Avenue was a cul-de-sac of modern bungalows. Hook peered at the street map and tried to decipher the lettering as Lambert swung the big Vauxhall through new building developments. If he had to hold the print any further away, his arms would not be long enough. 'Should be the next left, I think,' he said without conviction.

It was a quiet little close. From the end of it, a footpath by a tranquil stream took one to the centre of Oldford in less than five minutes. Perhaps Emily Godson's mother had thought her daughter would find this a more convenient as well as a more valuable residence than the old cottage as the years advanced.

Aunt Alice's smiling face was at the window when they parked, as if she was as anxious as they were to establish her niece's alibi for the night of the murder. They refused more tea and prevailed upon her to sit down with them on the comfortable chintz suite in the light and airy lounge. Everything was very neat: perhaps the home help had not long been gone. Alice Franklyn had the wide bright eyes and perpetual smile, the too-mobile hands, of a hyperactive child. Her cardigan, buttoned askew down its entire length, and a strand of grey hair wildly adrift of the rest hinted that all might not be well within that benign and venerable head.

'What a beautiful bungalow!' said Hook conventionally as they sat down.

'Mary bought it. Clever girl, Mary,' said the fey old lady. She rocked a little with mirth. They managed to establish that Mary was her sister and Emily Godson's mother. She spoke as though addressing her remarks not to them but to some imaginary person in the kitchen beyond, with whom she was sharing an innocent conspiracy. With difficulty, they steered the conversation towards Emily.

'Good girl, Emily. Comes round here to eat my cakes. Naughty, sometimes, but she's a good girl.' She leant towards them, close and confidential. 'Stanley knows. Stanley keeps her in order.' Suddenly she cackled with laughter, loud, strident and threatening. For a few seconds, she was transformed from child to witch. It was eerie and other-worldly, with the menace of the unknown behind it. In that moment, Bert Hook understood why an ignorant and superstitious peasantry would stoop to ducking-stools.

Then she was back to innocence again, smiling in childish conspiracy as Lambert guided her back towards Emily's visits. Hook felt a great sympathy, overlaid with the panic of one floundering out of his depth. Lambert could not dismiss thoughts of *Alice in Wonderland* as he strove to make sense of this modern namesake.

'So Emily comes here most evenings. Now, Alice, I want you to think very hard.' He tried not to think what sort of witness she would make: it would never come to that, surely. 'Can you remember last Wednesday evening? Take your time, now.'

The strange figure before him rocked back and forth on the settee several times, her furrowed brow simulating the thought he had instructed her to give to this intriguing puzzle. The broad smile never left the old, innocent face, the blue eyes glittered with the fun of superior knowledge as she looked up at the glass of the light fitting above them. She was like a child in possession of some immense secret, which in its revelation would make all these petty questions seem quite ludicrous.

'Oh yes, she was here,' she said. Her smile grew even broader at the recollection. Hook began to relax, Lambert smiled encouragement and wondered how to move on to specific times. Then Alice Franklyn went on, anxious to leave them in no doubt. 'She was here with her mother and her brother Michael. We had a nice family evening.' She folded her arms and hugged herself with the pleasure of the recollection. Then she began to check the carpet all round her feet with elaborate care.

In a rare moment of fantasy, stolid Bert Hook wondered if she could see the shattered pieces of her niece's alibi lying there.

CHAPTER EIGHTEEN

'Did you ever know Willy Harrison?' said Lambert to his wife. He studied the steam rising from the huge cup he always insisted on at breakfast, then looked beyond it to the blackbird he could see swaying gently on a rose in the back garden.

Christine wondered that a man should adopt a front so determinedly non-committal with his wife, making the partner of his bed a stranger over the breakfast table. She decided not to be insulted, for she understood far more clearly than he did himself the reason for this reserve, this awkwardness in what could have been a routine exchange. Lambert had a reluctance to talk about his work at home which amounted almost to a phobia, so that when as now he wished to draw upon some area of her knowledge, his manner had an obliquity more appropriate to the questioning of a stranger. Perhaps it went back to those near-forgotten days when they had almost split up, when she so resented his profession that she forbade it entry across her threshold, as some houseproud women forbid their husbands' muddy boots.

She watched him studiously avoiding her eye, resolutely studying the back garden in the morning sun, and felt a surge of tenderness for the gaucherie beneath the grey hairs. She said, 'He was Jim Harrison then. We began teaching together in the same year. That was in my grammar school days, of course.' She had re-trained for primary school teaching when she went back to work as their children grew. 'It seems an age ago now.'

She studied her husband's carefully assumed indifference with amusement that contained a nugget of irritation. He looked from blackbird to greenhouse, to the rowan tree at the far corner of the garden, but never at her. He waited for her to enlarge upon the subject of his question, and eventually she was drawn into his little game as she knew she would be. 'He was a good teacher, one of the very best. He knew kids instinctively—I don't think much of it came from training.' She paused, poured tea into her small cup, and said, 'I didn't like his wife.'

The abrupt disclosure made him glance at her at last, and they caught each other in their grins. For the first time, John Lambert realized the technique he had been using on his wife, and she caught the moment. Where twenty years ago there would have been mutual recriminations, there was now mutual amusement.

'She left him eventually,' said Lambert.

'I know. By that time I was pregnant with Sue and had left the school. One did, in those days.' For a moment, Lambert caught the scent of regret that she had not been around to console Jim Harrison when he needed her. Their own marriage had been shaky at just that time . . .

He concentrated on the material of his investigation. 'He was very depressed at the time of his divorce. Did he look round for consolation?'

If Christine Lambert thought the question in any way applied to herself, she gave no sign. She thought seriously with pursed lips before she said, 'I don't think so. Perhaps if he had done he wouldn't have had such a breakdown. There were plenty willing. He was an attractive man and a good teacher. You'd be surprised how attractive a combination that can be for young women.' Now it was she who looked down the garden, to where the same blackbird perched now on a mound of juniper to voice his full-throated diversion. Her neat brown hair, without a trace of grey yet, framed a profile which had the composure of a Renaissance Madonna. It was impossible to tell from her half-smile whether she was covering a small embarrassment or parodying her husband's recent attitude. Perhaps she merely disguised a great sadness. Just when he thought she had finished, she said, 'Emily Godson was one of them.'

After a few seconds of silence, she could not resist turning to examine the effects of her bombshell upon her husband. He said ruefully, 'You know I am investigating the staff of Freeman Estates, then?'

'Of course I do.' Her smile was the nearest thing to a verbal caress. Neither of them used 'dear' in their conversations, still less 'darling'. 'I'd have to be pretty stupid not to, with Stanley Freeman's death the local sensation and everyone probing me about your progress.'

'It was murder.' For him that was a revelation, but she dismissed it as an insult to her intelligence.

'I guessed that from your continued interest; and I do sometimes read the papers.

180

You may think that Emily Godson is on the way to becoming an old maid, but when Jim Harrison was disintegrating into Wino Willy she was an attractive woman.'

Lambert rallied before the feminist resentment he felt was imminent. 'On the contrary, I think she's an attractive woman still. If she finds it difficult to show herself as one, it may be because she's cared for a dying mother and a senile aunt better than any man could have.'

Christine inspected him wryly, her head on one side. He felt he had just about passed. She said, 'No doubt. Anyway, Emily was quite sweet on Jim, without eliciting a lot of response. Perhaps she still is. She was up on the moor last Sunday near Willy's hideout.'

If she knew she had tossed in a second grenade, she gave no sign. She was spreading marmalade thinly across a small piece of toast, with a concentration which argued it was her sole concern in the world. Lambert registered that she had known of Willy's remote lair on the moor when he himself had not. Perhaps he should ask her for information more regularly. 'Did you actually see her with Willy?'

'No. For all I know, Willy might not have been around himself. I didn't go right up there: I was with Jacqui and the dog.' Their second daughter had a high-spirited golden retriever that needed watching when there were sheep about. Christine hesitated, then decided to offer, 'I rather think Emily takes him food sometimes: I've seen her up there with a shopping-bag, looking embarrassed.'

It might be no more than that: another kindly impulse from a woman who preferred to disguise her humanity. Perhaps offered this time with the residual warmth of an old flame. She had not mentioned it to him. But why should she have? He had not raised the subject of Wino Willy with her. The important thing was that he now knew she had some kind of contact with that strange injured mind up there which he was more than ever convinced had something to do with this death. What might a man who cared so little for his own future not do to repay old emotional debts?

Christine watched his conjecture with distaste. She put crockery noisily on the tray and said, 'I shall be late if I'm not quick. Corpses may wait patiently for superintendents, but thirty-three small people will cause all kinds of mayhem if Mrs Lambert is late.'

'I'll do that,' said her husband, removing the tray with a grandiloquent sweep. 'Before you go, do you know any of these names?'

She looked quickly down his list of suspects as she picked up her car keys. There was shock in her eyes as she glanced sharply into his face, for she was quite shrewd enough to know why he was interested in these people. And one of them she did know. 'Jane Davidson. I taught

182

her when she was ten, and I've kept some track of her movements since then.'

'Why would that be?'

She shrugged. 'Jane was a bit of a problem girl. One-parent family; not much money around.'

'She wasn't the girl you used to take our kids' shoes in for?' He realized that her simple goodness, her determination to help lame dogs, which had once annoyed him, now filled him with tenderness in its recollection.

Christine shook her head. 'No, nothing as bad as that with Jane. She was an able girl, but too disturbed to make the most of herself. She didn't do as well as she should have done when she got to secondary school. She's a good girl when you get through to her, but very stubborn. I must go!'

He watched her reverse her small white car down the drive with practised efficiency. She was between the high gateposts when she stopped and beckoned him urgently to her; no inspector would have dared to make such an imperious gesture. Lambert leapt forward like a sprinter.

'Good!' said Christine appreciatively. 'I didn't know you could still move so fast.'

'I "started like a guilty thing upon a fearful summons",' quoted Lambert breathlessly.

'Save those games for Sergeant Hook,' she said with mock-severity. She was trying to use banter to lighten the impact of what she was

183

going to say. 'What I stopped my chariot to tell you was that I think Jane Davidson was very sweet on Willy Harrison's son a few years ago. Right up to the time he was killed in that car crash. Whether she's still in touch with Willy now or not, I don't know. It should be easy enough to check.'

It should indeed. A chastened Superintendent determined not to neglect such obvious sources of information in future.

CHAPTER NINETEEN

'A desirable small modern detached residence in a sought-after area,' said Hook. He felt he was getting the hang of this estate agency business.

'With distant views of the rolling Cotswold Hills,' suggested Lambert, gesturing towards the strip of landscape visible between the roofs of the houses on the opposite side of the road. 'A peaceful ambience where today's young executive might relax after the stresses of a crowded working day.' This was getting near to police prejudice. He assembled his features into careful neutrality as the electric bell-chime reverberated behind the mock-Georgian portico.

Simon Hapgood came forward with hand outstretched and wide, professional smile, the move he had practised on several hundred prospective clients of Freeman Estates. Only the eyes, light blue, brilliant and wary, were untouched by any sign of pleasure.

'Do sit down,' he said, gesturing with wide-flung arm at the leather Chesterfield sofa in the neat, uncluttered lounge. They placed their large feet carefully on the parquet floor between the two white goatskin rugs. Hapgood tossed his deep-gold hair back from his eyes in what seemed a habitual gesture. Then he positioned himself carefully opposite them in a brass-studded armchair, and so that the light was directly behind him.

'I'm sorry I had to postpone our meeting yesterday; we had to change our plans,' said Lambert. He wondered how much this young man knew of Emily Godson and the strange half-world of her ageing aunt.

'No sweat,' said Hapgood automatically: Lambert hoped his wince was not physical. The young man placed his right ankle carefully across his left knee in a gesture designed to show how relaxed he felt. Bert Hook made the mental note of 'public school' which was his own form of bias, resolving to check out this presumption later. He would have been surprised to know that Lambert, so cool and neutral on the surface, was having to resist a hope that this handsome, slightly effete young man would turn out to be their killer.

'How long have you been with Freeman

Estates?' he began, without further preparation.

'Two years. Just over,' said Hapgood. He looked at his watch, decided it was too early yet to suppress a yawn; this was stuff he'd already been over in the preliminary inquiries.

'You're happy with the firm?'

'I think I've been quite successful,' said Hapgood; his smile revealed the full glory of his dentistry.

'I said happy, though.' Lambert's smile just stopped short of mimicry of Hapgood's dazzling effort.

'I think I've settled in quite well.' Lambert waited patiently, letting his silence this time make the point. Hapgood was certainly not as comfortable as he pretended. A more confident opponent would have left it at that and forced further prompting. Perhaps it was Hook's deliberately elaborate recording of his words that rattled him into going on. 'What's happiness, after all? It's a job, a job I think I do well. I know the property market round here. I'm good at selling. In a more go-ahead firm, I'd be doing even better.' He stopped with a nervous little laugh. His desire to push himself must be habitual by now, if he chose to indulge it even in this context.

Lambert was carefully ignorant as he said, 'You don't think Freeman Estates has moved with the times?'

'It's a cut-throat business nowadays. The

best will thrive, the worst will go to the wall. That's how I like it.' Lambert wondered how much substance there was behind this bravado: he was aware that he was always prone to under-estimate those who spoke in clichés. Unintelligence did not always accompany insensitivity.

'So you think the procedures of the firm are not up to date?' he said innocently. He knew where he was steering.

Hapgood was looking like a man who wished he had not ventured into these waters. 'Sometimes one has to cut a few corners,' he said sourly. He had his right hand placed over his left upon his crossed thigh. The middle finger began to tap a silent, irregular rhythm.

'But not everyone is willing to do that?'

'Stanley Freeman did.' It was the reaction of a small man driven into a corner; Lambert did no more than raise his eyebrows. 'Stanley was swift enough on his feet when he saw the chance of a quick buck. There are ways and means in this business, Superintendent.' It was pathetic really, thought Hook, the way modern youth thought knowledge of the seamier side of life was closed to others, even policemen.

'Like cultivating old ladies with their own properties?' said Lambert.

It was as if Simon Hapgood had been hit in the face. His cheeks flushed red and his eyes filled with alarm for a moment at the knowledge that he had underestimated them.

'You know about Emily's Aunt Alice?' He could not keep his voice even.

'Among other things,' said Lambert shamelessly.

'It's Emily's own fault,' said Hapgood defensively. 'She should have known Freeman well enough. She's been there twenty years. Stuffy old biddy.' Lambert wondered what schemes of Simon's the sturdy Emily had refused to condone.

'What do you think of Miss Godson?' said Lambert.

'We haven't a lot in common,' said Hapgood, desperately simulating a neutrality which was too late.

'This is a murder inquiry,' Lambert reminded him impatiently, preparing to turn the screw a little tighter. 'At the moment there appear to be five people who could have committed this crime, including yourself. The innocent, as they say, have nothing to fear. Naturally, I am interested in your views on the other four, which will of course be treated as confidential. I shall in due course be asking them about you. Indeed, I have already heard some interesting assessments of everyone concerned.'

Hapgood, as he had anticipated, did not relish that thought. His mind must be reeling; Lambert had watched him mentally enumerating the other four suspects. Surely he must have divined by now that Denise

188

Freeman was the fifth possibility. Lambert said quietly, 'I gather that you don't get on with Emily Godson.' He was prepared to prompt now that his quarry had been driven into the desired area of questioning.

'She doesn't like *me*. Self-righteous cow.' He muttered the last words, then glanced up guiltily as he considered the impression he was creating. The public school veneer had been precious thin, thought Hook, with his own self-righteousness. 'You must understand that I'm younger than Emily, and enthusiastic to succeed. She's done nothing but put obstacles in my way. It took her a long time to become a Senior Negotiator and she doesn't want to see anyone else moving up rapidly.'

Probably there was something in it, Lambert thought. If Emily had met old-fashioned male prejudice, she would be scarcely human if she was not jealous of early preferment for someone like Simon. Especially if his progress was built on unscrupulous short cuts, as he had already half-admitted it was.

'Do you think Miss Godson killed Stanley Freeman?' he asked simply. He felt Hook shift beside him on the sofa: it was a highly irregular question. He was more interested in Hapgood's reaction than his opinion.

He tossed his head again, the sun behind him gilding his hair into an incongruous halo. He pursed his soft, small lips and folded his arms, as if giving the proposition serious

189

thought. 'I suppose she could have. She'd certainly no reason to love the boss.' Then he brightened, as if a notion had suddenly struck him. It was impossible to be certain whether it really was a new idea, or something he had thought of earlier and was now eager to plant. 'She knows all about EXIT. I remember her going on to us about people's right to die with dignity and the good work EXIT was doing.'

'When was this?' said Lambert, carefully unexcited. He wished he could see Hapgood's face more clearly.

'Oh, a while ago. Six months, maybe more. She had their literature; I think she was going to join.'

In other words, Emily Godson had become interested in the harrowing question of how best to die after the long trauma of her mother's illness, when her aunt's senile dementia was becoming more marked. It was natural enough, but an area of questioning to be explored when he saw her again: the society's material had clearly stimulated the idea of an ingenious murder in someone. Denise Freeman was the only one he had questioned about EXIT. He tried not to find Hapgood's eagerness to incriminate a colleague distasteful.

'George Robson?' he said abruptly.

Hapgood was surprised but not thrown off balance by the sudden shift. His quick eyes switched back and forth between

190

Superintendent and Sergeant, looking for any indication of where their suspicions lay. 'I wouldn't think so,' he said eventually.

'Mr Hapgood, I'm not asking you now to speculate about the culprit. I am looking for extra facts which may be significant. Things you may know but which we may not have discovered yet. You will hardly need telling that it is your duty to help us in this way.'

Hapgood looked sullen. 'I don't know anything about George Robson which would make him a killer. He didn't like Stanley Freeman, but none of us did.' He stopped, aware that the wrong pronoun had slipped out.

'You didn't like Mr Freeman yourself?' said Lambert, wondering if he sounded smug. Hapgood looked carefully at the coffee table between them and said nothing.

Then Bert Hook, making one of his rare interventions, struck below the belt with ruthless precision. 'You used to call him Joe Stalin, I believe?' he said, without even looking up from his notes.

Hapgood reddened: his face was as revealing in this respect as a young girl's. 'I didn't mean anything by it. It was just a joke. I—I was letting off steam when he wasn't there.' They could see him conjecturing about who had revealed this. Lambert would be interested to know himself in due course; it was something Hook had picked up from the preliminary interviews by others.

'Quite,' said Lambert drily. He succeeded in making a perfectly natural reaction, the kind of safety-valve many employees indulge in in the boss's absence, sound sinister. He was quite enjoying the embarrassment of this young popinjay. But that was an indulgence, unless he could use it in the rest of the interrogation.

'He piled work on to me. Arranged appointments in the evening that he should have taken himself. He was exploiting me . . .' Lambert let him run on with the petty catalogue. It was probably largely true, from what he had pieced together of the dead man, but hardly a motive for murder. Hopgood went on rather desperately with his self-justification, until the Superintendent wondered if he had some other, more real motive that he wanted to conceal. He let the petty list of grievances run out, feeling like an actor trying to time a good line perfectly.

Then he said, 'Where were you on that Wednesday night?' He was pleased with the effect he achieved. The blood drained from Simon Hapgood's face as quickly as it had risen earlier. His eyes widened as he tried to divine what was going on behind Lambert's impassive features. He must surely have expected to have to account for his movements on the night of the murder, but the abrupt appearance of the question in the midst of his evasions had thrown him off balance.

'I—I was expecting to go to Lydon Hall. Then Stanley said he would show the Harbens round himself. They were important clients. He was good with Americans, he said.'

'And you weren't?'

This time Hapgood refused to rise to the bait. 'Perhaps not as good as Stanley. He could he very persuasive with important people, when he chose.' It was the second time they had heard this grudging acknowledgement of the dead man's expertise: George Robson had said more or less the same thing. It marked a measure of recovery in Simon Hapgood. He was pleased with himself for his compliment to Stanley Freeman, as if he had compensated for his vituperative Joe Stalin nickname by this evidence of balance. He plucked the creases of his trousers precisely into position and worked hard at looking thoroughly composed.

'You haven't told me where you were on Wednesday evening yet,' Lambert reminded him.

Hapgood produced a packet of tipped cigarettes. He offered them to his interlocutors, was refused, took one himself. He lit it with a butane lighter, pressed his shoulders against the back of his chair, blew a contemplative funnel of smoke at the ceiling. It was a caricature of relaxation and clear conscience. But as he arranged packet and lighter on the coffee table between them, the lighter slipped from his hands and clattered unnaturally loud upon the table's smooth brown surface, destroying completely the effect he had striven so hard to create. Hook felt like jeering as he had when a small boy at a villain's mistake in the cinema, but his solemn mask never slipped as he waited with ballpoint over his notebook.

Hapgood said, 'I had a viewing of Milton Farm at six-thirty. I was rather at a loose end after I had left the clients. I had something to eat here and then went out to a pub, the Stonemasons' Arms in Cornbrook.' It was a well-known pub in a village three miles from Oldford, fashionable with the affluent younger drinkers; the car park was a perpetual temptation to thieves, with its sprinkling of Porsches and BMWs. It was within a mile and a half of Lydon Hall through the lanes: three minutes' drive for a man in a hurry.

'Timing?' This was Hook, flicking over a new page in his notebook and making it clear that every word would be recorded and checked out.

Hapgood paused, took his time: Lambert suddenly had the feeling that he had rehearsed all this. 'I can't be sure. I must have come back here about seven. I used the microwave to heat a frozen dinner for one, so I didn't take very long over it. I expect I was in the pub by about eight o'clock, but I couldn't be certain. I was relaxing. I didn't know at the time it would be important.' The sentence they had heard so

194

often before. That was because it was true, of course. But the story had come out just too glibly.

'You stayed there until closing time?'

'More or less. About half past ten, I think.'

'No doubt you saw people you knew who could vouch for your presence there.'

If it was a challenge, it did not ruffle him. 'One or two. I'm quite well known there.' He reeled off three names, again just too quickly for the recollection to be spontaneous. But it would be a foolish man who had not reviewed his movements on that fateful evening.

Bert Hook wrote down the names laboriously, spreading the seconds to build the tension. Then he said, 'What car do you drive, Mr Hapgood?'

Was there a snatch of breath before he replied? It might have been no more than the surprise of an innocent man at an unexpected question.

'A Ford Sierra.'

'Colour?'

'Dark blue. Not metallic.'

Hook wrote down the words while Lambert studied the fresh young face intently. They stood up. Hapgood's relief was evident. He even attempted a grotesque return to his manner at the outset of the interview. 'Well, gentlemen, if I can be of any further help—'

'What do you know about Denise Freeman?' Lambert spat the question like a poisoned dart. He was surprised at the hostility in his own voice.

Hapgood, rising to shepherd them off the premises, had turned towards the door, so that the light at last fell full upon his face. They watched the pale, epicene features fighting for control. The eyelids blinked three, four times in rapid succession, the small lips twitched twice before he managed to speak. His first words emerged as little more than a croak.

'Why do you ask me about her?'

Both men watched him struggling for control, excited by a reaction far greater than either had anticipated. There was a pause of no more than two seconds, which seemed much longer to all of them. Then Lambert said coldly, 'Because she is a suspect, just as George Robson and Emily Godson are. As you are yourself. As Jane Davidson is.' He watched Hapgood closely as he produced the last name. There was nothing like the reaction which Denise Freeman's name had produced. For a moment then there had been real fear. For himself, or for the enigmatic widow? Lambert's question had been provoked by his remembrance of a single, unreturned look Hapgood had directed to Denise Freeman across the coffin of the murdered man.

Hapgood might have blustered if he could have managed more control of himself. As it was, he was wise or fortunate enough to say nothing. Lambert, anxious to keep him reeling, to prevent the retreat into his legal right to say nothing, volunteered, 'Mrs Freeman has provided us with an account of her whereabouts on the evening of the murder, as you have. As Sergeant Hook has just indicated to you, we look for witnesses to corroborate all such statements. So far, we have found none to substantiate Mrs Freeman's story.'

Hapgood's eyes flicked to Lambert's face, then to Hook's; he found no clue in either to help him. They saw fear in the bright blue eyes; the bright room seemed unnaturally silent.

'Do you know of any reason why Mrs Freeman should kill her husband?'

Hapgood shook his head, dumb and miserable. Neither of them thought him altruistic enough for it to be a detached concern about an innocent woman.

'Have you any idea where she was last Wednesday night?'

'No!' This time the response was loud, instinctive, an emotional reaction rather than a refusal of information. He must have realized how odd it sounded in the pause which followed. He swallowed hard, then said unsteadily, 'I went to the pub as I said. I didn't see Denise.'

'I hadn't suggested you did,' said the Superintendent quietly. He wondered if Hapgood was too nervous now to realize how much he had given away in that single unguarded use of the Christian name. For the first time, Lambert was toying with the idea that these two had indeed been with each other at the time of the murder. Perhaps, indeed, at the scene of the murder. 'Now, I must ask you this, Mr Hapgood. Have you anything further to tell us which might bear on the death of Stanley Freeman?' He made it as simple and as unbending as he could, as though he were enunciating a formal charge.

'No. Nothing. You must believe me.' Hapgood tossed the golden hair back in his habitual gesture and attempted the look of appealing sincerity his nerves could not sustain. Lambert's eyes never left his face.

'We shall need to talk further,' he said. 'Probably after I've seen Mrs Freeman again. You won't be leaving the area, will you, Mr Hapgood?' It was more a directive than a question.

Hapgood shook his head miserably, then stood in the Georgian doorway until Lambert had reversed the Vauxhall and driven out of sight. Then he went hopelessly back inside and shut the front door carefully. He picked up the nearly spent cigarette, drew a last nervous comfort from it as he tapped out the digits on the phone.

It rang three, four times. As it was answered, he stubbed out the butt of the cigarette.

CHAPTER TWENTY

The police station at Oldford was in a chronically overcrowded Victorian building. Plans were in hand to remedy the situation. Within two years, a disused primary school would be converted to allow the burgeoning force the space it needed. Crime has overtaken fecundity as a feature of rural England.

But serious crime was still mercifully rare here. This meant that the CID section was even more cramped than the rest. The murder room had been established in a terrapin building in the yard behind the station, the only place where the required resources could be concentrated efficiently. Eight days into the inquiry, Superintendent Lambert reviewed progress with DI Rushton and DS Hook.

The routine business of the investigation had continued steadily, the machinery of police routine forming a background to Lambert's less predictable procedures. Here were stored the signed statements of the discoverers of the corpse and the people who had subsequently emerged as major suspects. Fingerprints from the drawing-room at Lydon Hall were filed alongside those of the suspects. In plastic bags were the minutiæ of hairs, pins and clothing fibres, all meticulously labelled. Out of sight but even more carefully packaged were the shoes and clothes of the dead man, waiting for the recovery elsewhere of the tiniest fibres which might indicate a connection between murderer and victim on that fateful night. They were folded carefully, filed in plastic sheeting in the drawers of an old cabinet, out of sight lest they should distress close relatives. In another drawer were the plastic bag which had enclosed the corpse's head and the suicide note found in the pocket, waiting to become in due course Exhibits A and B in court.

It would never do for a spouse to set eyes on such grisly reminders of the crime. Unless of course she was simply being confronted with her own evil deed. Lambert was dissatisfied with his picture of the widow of the late Stanley Freeman. He had checked the pages of the preliminary interviews, Hook's notes on their own exchanges, and the findings from the subsequent checks he had ordered. His *amour propre* was disturbed: Denise Freeman had so far revealed to them little more than she had chosen to. He saw her in his mind's eye, cool, dark and Gallic, her Mona Lisa smile seeming to suggest her superiority to the simple techniques of the English police. She had seemed both calm and ruthless in her assessments of others during their interview. She would make a good murderer, if she thought such desperate measures necessary. Or—and the thought which had been buried in

200

the recesses of his mind suddenly sprang clear—she was the kind of woman who could persuade men to kill for her.

'Denise Freeman said that on the night of the murder she was at the cinema in Tewkesbury. Any corroboration yet?' He thought of the widow's cool, detailed account of *The Last Emperor* and its stars, so matter-of-fact and convincing as they had sat on her manicured lawns.

Rushton knew without looking at the reports of his detective-constables. 'Nothing yet. There were two front of house staff and an usherette in the cinema: none of them remember her. The place was almost full.' Of course. It would be for a popular film; this woman, if she was trying to deceive them, would no doubt have taken account of that.

'Any of them male?' A red-blooded man was more likely to remember those dark eyes and lustrous black tresses.

'Only the house manager. He spent a lot of the evening checking takings.'

'What about her car?'

'A green Volvo. A better chance of someone seeing a car like that than a Ford or a Vauxhall. But no sighting recorded yet. Of course, she says she left it in the public car park.'

'And of course she conveniently went nowhere except to the cinema. No snack, no drinks?'

Rushton shrugged his shoulders. 'It's a long film, which would occupy most of the evening. And she was a woman on her own.' Both reasons why she should not dally in Tewkesbury, certainly. The fact that no one could so far confirm her alibi might not be significant: no one had seen her elsewhere either. Somehow, she did not seem the kind of woman who would habitually visit the cinema alone, as she claimed. Had she been with anyone else on that Wednesday evening?

'What progress on George Robson's story?'

'More to report there.' Rushton was glad to have something more positive as evidence of the team's industry. 'He was seen up on the common that night with his dog.'

Lambert should have been relieved to find one at least of his suspects being eliminated. In fact, he had been remembering the way he had seen Robson eyeing Denise Freeman at the funeral, and toying with a lurid hypothesis involving them as joint murderers. Reluctantly, he abandoned the notion.

'What exactly did he say to us about his movements, Bert?' he asked Hook. Rushton, anxious to give chapter and verse to his findings, was left to cool his heels while the Sergeant thumbed ponderously to the right page in his notes, then enunciated his summary as clearly as if he was in court. 'He was up on the common with Fred, the labrador. He says he always is between eight and nine in the summer. He couldn't remember actually speaking to anyone on that night, though he often does. He and Fred went right up on to the moor because the dog had been in all day. Fred was chasing rabbits, but he never catches any,' he ended inconsequentially.

'That tallies with our witnesses,' said Rushton, his tone just edging his impatience with the delay. He was young for a detective-inspector, still without a grey hair, his face almost unlined; he played things carefully by the book, but knew when and how the book could help him. Before too long, thought Lambert, I shall be out to grass and replaced by someone like him. He tried to welcome the idea, failed, and was irked by his own pettiness.

Rushton thumbed through his own pages, arriving at the right one much more quickly than Hook, speaking with no more than an occasional confirmatory glance downwards. He was on top of this, his demeanour said.

'DC Sampson has found three people who saw him up there. None of them actually spoke to him, because he was too far away, but they waved and Robson waved back. They all know Fred, because he's a character among dogs, apparently. Among other things, a right randy bugger. Two of our sightings had bitches.' How straightforwardly these things were arranged in the canine world; if the couplings and aspirations of the human participants in this case were only so manifest, all might swiftly be illuminated. 'Fred went away with his master up on to the moor, diverting his energy into chasing the wildlife as Robson said.'

'What was Robson wearing?'

'Old trilby, green wellies, sports jacket. The gear he always wears for walking the dog: we've checked it out.' Rushton was glad to have been asked, and thus allowed to demonstrate the diligence of the work he was orchestrating.

'Wellies on a summer evening?' said Hook.

'Dog-walkers tend to stick to what is comfortable, summer and winter,' said Rushton, who had a dog himself. 'It seems to be what Robson always wears; we saw the clothes at his house.' Lambert nodded, recalling Robson dressed exactly thus when he returned to his house with Fred to find them waiting to interview him.

'What about Emily Godson?' he said. To Rushton, who had expected some recognition of his efficient dismissal of Robson from their list of possible murderers, it seemed almost a snub. He took a deep breath before reporting what Lambert already knew. 'She says she was at the house of her aunt, Alice Franklyn. DC Pearson says her aunt supports this, but that it wouldn't stand up in court.' Rushton looked at his notes in some puzzlement.

'DC Pearson shows a mastery of

understatement that could take him to high rank,' said Lambert with a dry smile. 'Bert and I found her quite charming, but as nutty as a Brazilian barmcake. Emily could have used her for that very reason if she was desperate. For what it's worth, I think Emily is bright enough to arrange a more reliable alibi if she was our killer.'

'Has she a wide circle of friends, sir?' said Rushton. He felt as if he was trying to retrieve lost ground. His Superintendent left the reply to Bert Hook, with the benefits of his local knowledge.

'She's lived in the area all her life, and worked at Freeman Estates for over thirty years. She must know most of the locals. I doubt whether she has many really close friends among them, though.'

Rushton tried not to sound too eager. 'It's possible, then, that she hadn't too many options in framing an alibi. We're saying that the story that she was with her aunt isn't worth a lot. From where she stands, it may simply look impossible to disprove.'

Lambert felt he was being corrected on an obvious point: suspects did not have to prove their innocence. He wondered if his vague desire to discomfort Rushton came from anything more than resentment of his relative youth. 'All right. In our terms, Emily Godson goes down at present as having no satisfactory alibi.' How gruff and grudging he sounded. He was glad Christine could not see him managing his team: schoolteachers were too ready with applications of amateur psychology. 'What about young Mr Hapgood?'

'Not quite so young as he appears at first sight, sir. Simon Hapgood is thirty. We've been digging a little.' Rushton was back in his stride now. From widely divergent sources, they had built a better background to the recently promoted Senior Negotiator than any of the others. They had listened to gossip, examined his application form for his original post with Freeman Estates, enlisted the Sussex CID to enquire discreetly into his previous career.

'Hapgood left his public school without taking A-levels, under something of a cloud. The head, now retired, says he was "not a good influence" on the other boys. He hinted at homosexuality, but there is no subsequent record of it. Either it was a stage in adolescence, or what he was expelled for was more a combination of factors.'

'Drugs?' said Lambert. He was aware that Rushton was making a meal of this, and absurdly delighted to see him deflated by the anticipation of his next revelation. This was an efficient colleague he was needling: he tried unsuccessfully to feel guilty.

'Indeed yes, sir. Hapgood was bound over at Hastings eighteen months later. Possession of cannabis and LSD. No suggestion of trafficking. Arrested at a party.' He offered each detail as if making a plea of mitigation in court. Rushton, for all his consciousness of rank, was not much older than Hapgood. Perhaps attitudes to the drug culture were conditioned by age as well as occupation. 'He seems to have learned his lesson, in that respect, anyway. There is no subsequent connection with hard drugs.' Lambert thought of Hapgood's trembling hands as they caressed a cigarette in the final stages of their meeting; perhaps it was just that his drug dependence now was legal.

Rushton went on with his carefully gleaned information before there could be any more inspired guesses from his chief. 'After a series of jobs in small firms, possibly obtained by his father's influence in the area, Hapgood had three years with a firm of stockbrokers in Brighton.'

'Why did he leave?' Failure was always more interesting to policemen than success.

'He left under a cloud.' Rushton ruefully acknowledged that he had been anticipated again. 'There were some rather dubious share-dealings on his own account and a suggestion that he was unloading dubious shares from one client to another. He was warned, and apparently desisted. What finally sent him on his way was an attempt at what the broking fraternity call "insider dealing": using confidential information for personal profit at the expense of the public. The Fraud Squad spend untold hours on it in the City at the moment, as you know. Hapgood was a boy in a man's world, attempting to use a London contact to get in on the act.'

'And no doubt he got caught while the big lads got away. Was there a prosecution?' said Lambert, knowing the answer even as he spoke. The people who screamed for convictions were often the last to pursue prosecutions when it was inconvenient.

'No, sir. He was sacked, but as usual the firm said there wasn't enough evidence for a court case. Which means, of course, that they're an old-established firm who wouldn't want that kind of publicity and a loss of confidence among colonels retiring with their gratuities.' Superintendent and Inspector were united at last in their moment of ritual resentment against an uncaring public. It enabled Rushton to continue with greater relaxation.

'Hapgood moved to a rather dubious financial services firm in Hampshire, who have since gone out of business. He was plugging speculative investments at high rates of interest. He seems to have pushed things a bit too far even among those chancers, because he was sent on his way just before they packed up.'

'No form?'

'Not apart from the early LSD.'

'Any violence?'

'None at all that we've been able to find.' Yet this death, with its subtle, quiet suffocation, disguised as an EXIT suicide, was in a way non-violent. No bludgeoning with a blunt instrument, no blowing a man's head away. Just a quiet, ruthless dispatch into eternity. Was he rationalizing because of his dislike of Hapgood?

'Sexual inclinations?'

'Women. Consistently. None of them for very long. Whether he prefers it that way, or whether they tire of him, is not very clear. Perhaps both.'

Simon Hapgood was not so uncommon a type in police experience, after all. With an education and obvious good looks, they lived on their wits in their twenties. If successful, they became with experience and discretion successful businessmen in their thirties, then pillars of a society in which wealth was the easiest measure. If they failed, they often declined into seedy confidence-tricksters in middle age, preying on the gullible young housewives and elderly widows who lived in the unreal world of cheap romances.

John Lambert had a sudden fantasy which involved the active body of the fair-haired, blue-eyed Mr Hapgood. Perhaps he had settled to life at Freeman Estates, even if he occasionally pushed its possibilities to a point only just within the law. But he surely did not live a life of monastic seclusion in that aseptic lounge of his. Lambert wished he had seen the decor of the bedroom. Before the thought could induce too much excitement in a middle-aged superintendent, he turned briskly to Hook, that bromide among sergeants.

'Did you check his story with the pub, Bert?'

'I did better than that. I found witnesses.' Hook was human enough to change to a more brisk delivery in response to Rushton's efforts. 'The landlord at the Stonemasons' Arms in Cornbrook confirms he was there that Wednesday night. They were quite busy and he can't be sure about times. He remembers Hapgood ordering a round of drinks at what he thinks was about nine-thirty, because Hapgood was quite boisterous about it. He had the impression he'd been there for some time, but he couldn't he sure of that. But Hapgood gave us the names of three people who'd been with him, and I've spoken to two of them. They confirm his presence, but they can't be precise about the time we know is important.'

He flicked the leaves of his notebook and found the names he wanted with unaccustomed celerity. 'Julian Armitage remembers Hapgood ordering that round of drinks as soon as he joined their little group. He gave them the impression he'd already been in the pub for some time with other people before coming over to them, but when I pressed him for names he hadn't actually seen anyone: it's possible the idea is no more than a notion planted by Hapgood. Hazel Smythe-Walker is even less use: she joined the group at about nine forty-five, and can vouch for the fact that Hapgood stayed with them until closing time, but she obviously can't know about the time of his arrival. She thought Hapgood had had a few and been there for quite some time, but that again might be no more than an impression he worked to create. Incidentally, Hapgood might have been working on his alibi since the murder. He's been back to the pub three times in the last week, each time from eight o'clock onwards.'

Lambert, who now thought he knew where Hapgood had been for at least some part of that Wednesday night, had not yet an iota of proof. He leaned forward to Rushton, all differences forgotten in the excitement of a new idea. 'How many of the staff of Freeman Estates were involved with Lydon Hall?'

Rushton was shrewd enough to pick up his chief's train of thought quickly; his own agitation rose as he replied. 'Only Stanley Freeman, I think. He handled the whole thing himself, even the measuring for the brochure. Robson and Hapgood seemed quite put out, but thought they'd get their chance at a sale if it didn't go immediately.'

'So as far as we know, only Freeman ever visited the place officially. It has a gravel drive to the front and both sides. Has anyone checked the tyres of our suspects for traces of gravel?'

Rushton shook his head dumbly, wondering how to frame his excuse. But Lambert was too excited to pause now. 'Damn! My fault entirely. The old gardener told us the first day we were up there that Freeman had done all the measuring of house and garden himself. I just assumed with a property of that size and importance that most of them would have been up there at some time.'

'I think we all did,' said Rushton miserably. He was only too conscious that they had cast aside one of the few bonuses offered to them in a difficult case. He could think of only one fact to offer, and that a negative one. 'I think Denise Freeman went up there with her husband. She was interested in seeing the Hall and its furnishings, and Freeman couldn't shut her out as he did his employees.'

Lambert said, 'Check the tyres of the other four now. If they have good tyres—and as they're all company cars they probably have— there might even be traces of gravel after eight days. Get a sample of Lydon Hall gravel to Forensic right away and tell the lab boys to test the tyre samples against it; top priority. Check Hapgood's tyres particularly carefully: it's a blue Sierra. Possibly the car seen by the Harbens, but we need more proof than they can offer us.'

'How openly?' Rushton was anxious for the

relief afforded by action, but cautious still, as appropriate for a man steadily on the way up.

'It doesn't matter. The staff of Freeman Estates park their cars in the public car park behind their office. If they see uniformed men checking tyre-treads, I don't mind stirring things up a bit. Pity we can't observe their reactions; Hapgood's in particular.'

Rushton made a full and careful note: if there were subsequent questions about irregularities in procedure, it would be as well to make it clear they were on the Superintendent's initiative. He picked up a phone and set his detective-constables to work, while his chief brooded darkly about missed opportunities. Then Rushton cleared his throat, received Lambert's affirmative nod, and moved to his next typewritten sheet.

'Jane Davidson,' he announced.

'We haven't even seen her yet. Anything for us to follow up?' In his own mind, Lambert considered her the least likely of their suspects. As yet, they had found no obvious motive for the receptionist at Freeman Estates to kill her employer. Both Denise Freeman and Emily Godson had noticed something strange in her relationship with Freeman, but it might have been no more than wishful thinking and a little spite. How much was his own view swayed by her sex and her youth? He remembered Christine's assertion that there was a good girl lurking beneath a recalcitrant exterior. But experience should have taught him by now to dismiss no one as a possibility until he had built up a careful factual picture. He was anxious to reduce the field: perhaps too anxious.

Rushton said, 'She claims she was at home with her mother on the night of the murder. Not the kind of alibi I like. I saw the mother myself. She bears out everything her daughter says and probably it's fair enough. But there's something odd about both of them; I felt things were being held back. What bits we've been able to find support her story. The neighbour is a spinster who sees most of the comings and goings by day.'

'By day?'

'Until her television goes on. Which it does at about seven o'clock on most nights. She saw young Jane come in about six. She didn't see her go out, but I doubt if she'd have noticed once she was glued to *Coronation Street.*' It was true enough: people heard rather than saw the movements of their neighbours at nights and once the ubiquitous chatter of television and radio took over, little else was heard, a fact of great assistance to the criminal fraternity.

'There is one interesting thing. It was Jane Davidson who took the phone message which put the viewing time for the Harbens back from eight-thirty to nine. She says it was a female voice she did not recognize— presumably Mrs Harben, since the change

214

was genuine.'

'But I assume she told Stanley Freeman?' said Lambert, trying to work through the implications.

'He wasn't in the office.'

'Car phone?'

'No. Stanley Freeman didn't think it was worthwhile in a small local business. I suspect he didn't have one because he didn't want to be contacted when he was away from the office.' They paused for a moment, thinking of the sad figure of Margot Jones in Gloucester; she scarcely seemed to warrant any title as glamorous as mistress. 'Jane Davidson left a message on Freeman's Ansafone at home. It was cleared before we got there. Denise Freeman said she didn't run it until the next day and cleared it then. It means she could have known the night before, of course.'

There was silence in the Murder Room while they weighed the possibilities. Anyone who knew the viewing had been postponed would have had half an hour to meet the unsuspecting Freeman, perhaps ply him with whisky to supplement the hip flask they had found in his car, complete the murder. Lambert wondered if the others felt the frisson of excitement he experienced now and had known before at key moments in investigations.

'Who else knew?'

'Jane thinks no one at Freeman Estates.

Robson and Hapgood were both out with clients at the time of the phone call. That's genuine enough: the viewings are booked down and we've checked them. Emily Godson was in the office but not around when Jane took the phone call—either making tea in the kitchen or out at the washroom. I hardly think a conspiracy between those two is likely: they're like chalk and cheese.'

'Jane knew herself, of course,' said Lambert. 'So far, she's the only one who we know for certain had the knowledge and could have used it. Did she take any other steps to try to inform Stanley Freeman of the changed time?'

'She left a note of the change on Freeman's desk. As she says, she left messages in two places and couldn't have done much more. At the time it seemed that the worst that could happen would be that if Freeman didn't get the message he'd have to kick his heels and wait at Lydon Hall.'

'Do we have the note?'

Rushton shook his head. He was glad to be questioned in such detail; as in the case of Simon Hapgood, his thoroughness was being revealed.

'No. George Robson says it wasn't there when he cleared Freeman's desk next day. We checked the waste-paper baskets and the dustbin outside. Nothing.'

Lambert shut his eyes and thought hard. Three possibilities: first, Jane Davidson had not in fact left any note; second, Freeman had found it but still gone to Lydon Hall at around the original time, perhaps to an assignation with his killer; third, it had been removed by some person anxious to conceal the change from the murder victim. It could have course have been placed by Jane Davidson herself but removed after she had checked that Freeman had not been in to see it. According to her story, she was the one person who knew for certain of the changed time. Except that . . . He stopped that train of thought before it got still more convoluted.

He thought of Jane Davidson at the funeral, standing stiff and motionless in her high-heeled shoes and high-necked black dress, red nails bright against the shiny black handbag. She had looked young and vulnerable, in need of a lead in graveside behaviour. But there had been more satisfaction than grief as she looked down at the coffin in its final pit.

'Did Jane Davidson strike you as a murderer?' And does that question sound as banal to you as it does to me, he thought, as soon as he had framed it.

Apparently not, for Rushton was frowning his way to a considered reply. 'Not immediately,' he said eventually. 'But she's a hard young miss. A little older than she looks —twenty-four, I think. No father, used to looking out for herself. We didn't turn up any motive, but both she and her mother seemed scared. As I told you, we felt they were hiding something, but we couldn't find out what. It's possible they'd agreed the story about her alibi, but we couldn't shake them on it. Simple enough tale, of course. Jane washed her hair, Mrs Davidson made a cake, they both watched telly. Not much to trip them up there.'

True enough, and by now they would be well rehearsed, if indeed they were lying. Rushton's more objective investigations now supported Emily Godson's view that Jane was hiding something about her relationship with Freeman. Lambert made a mental note to explore this when they saw young Miss Davidson.

Suddenly, the phone shrilled at the far end of the room. It had done so twice before during their conference, yet this time DC Spencer felt all their eyes upon him as he answered.

'Yes. Yes . . . It could be . . . Is he with you now? Wait a minute, the Superintendent is here in the Murder Room now.' Finding Lambert at his side, he handed the phone to him. 'It's PC Standing from a patrol car, sir.'

The uniformed PC at the other end of the line was suddenly nervous at this unexpected link with top brass. 'It may be nothing at all, sir. I just thought we should ring in to the Murder Room.'

'Quite. Well?' The monosyllables scarcely calmed PC Standing.

'We're at Lydon Hall, sir. The scene of crime people said there was no point in leaving anyone here permanently, but we drive in and round the house as part of our routine until further notice.'

'And?'

'Well, we've just met someone. Round the back, in the woods. He's a kind of—'

'Wino Willy.'

'Yes, sir. You know him?' Relief at not having to attempt a description.

'I know him. Sergeant Hook and I interviewed him,' said Lambert, wondering if that wild oral *pas de deux* on the moor could be dignified as anything so formal.

'It was you he wanted to see,' said PC Standing, under-standing Willy's nonsense at last. He would not tell the Superintendent that Willy had asked for the Headmaster.

'Do you have him there?' said Lambert.

'No, sir. We tried to get him into the car, but he ran off into the woods.'

Despite his excitement, Lambert was glad Willy had not been manhandled. But he knew he must get to him; if Willy had tried to contact him he was prepared to speak now. And he was involved in this crime somewhere. All the suspects knew him, except possibly Simon Hapgood. George Robson must see him often on his daily walks with Fred on common and moor. Denise Freeman had known him well in the past and perhaps kept

219

in contact. Emily Godson took him supplies of food and had been up to his lair three days before the murder. Jane Davidson had been close to the only son whose death had pitched Willy's mind into the abyss. And Willy, he was sure, knew things about this death. Had almost told him things.

PC Standing was struggling with the most difficult part of his message. 'He—he said to tell you something, sir. It was in odd words—I couldn't make sense of it.'

'A quotation?' Suddenly Lambert knew this was crucial.

'Yes, sir, it probably was. I can't remember the actual words.'

'Try, Standing, unless you want to remain a PC for the next twenty years.'

Standing put his hand over the phone, consulted his colleague. When he came back to them he said hesitantly, 'Something about murder and a tongue, sir. And an organ . . .' His voice tailed away as he realized how feeble it sounded.

But he had given Lambert enough. The Superintendent could see Willy before him, hair wildly dishevelled, clothes in rags, eyes alight with pleasure as he offered the words of another sinewy mind that had gone astray. Willy, like that other beguiling tiddler, was mad but north-north-west: this lover of nature would certainly know a hawk from a handsaw. And Lambert had the quotation ' "For murder,

220

though it have no tongue, will speak with most miraculous organ,"' he said.

'That's it, sir,' said PC Standing, with surprise and admiration. He did not know that Willy had picked up the phrase with which he had concluded that headlong exchange on the moor, to signify that now he wished to speak.

Lambert was exultant. Wino Willy was going to give him his murderer.

CHAPTER TWENTY-ONE

'Have you found who did it yet?' said Jane Davidson as she sat down.

Perhaps it was just nervous bravado. Lambert was used to all kinds of reactions from those involved in serious crime inquiries.

'We have our ideas,' he said evenly. He afforded her the briefest smile possible at the outset of an interview.

He had arranged to see her in Stanley Freeman's old office. George Robson, the new incumbent, was out for the morning and had encouraged the use of this inner sanctum, which was almost soundproof. Lambert sat at the big desk in what must have been Freeman's swivel chair, with Hook impassive as a Buddha on his left. They saw no sign of discomfort in their subject. Miss Davidson disposed herself unhurriedly in the comfortable chair opposite the Superintendent, placed her handbag on the corner of the desk, experimentally crossed and uncrossed her legs, settled eventually into the attitude she chose. A phrase Lambert thought to have forgotten years ago came back to him: in his days of National Service, drill sergeants would have called this 'dumb insolence'. He watched her steadily; he could outsmart her easily enough at this game, where experience and rank were crushing attributes.

'You will appreciate that in a murder inquiry we have to investigate the backgrounds and movements of all those close to the deceased,' he said.

'If you like,' said Jane Davidson.

'I don't, always,' said Lambert heavily. 'It's my job, that's all.' It was the way he used to pick up his daughter in the worst period of her adolescence. He looked down at his notes: this girl was the same age as that daughter, who was now expecting her second child. Jane Davidson was a young woman, with experience of life and its passions, not a fractious child. Youth had energy, and the ruthlessness that often came from a tendency to think in blacks and whites, rather than shades of grey. He resolved to think of her as a potential murderer. Or at least an accessory to murder.

'Where were you on the night of this killing?' The abruptness made it sound almost an accusation; he would waste no further time on tact and explanations.

'I was at home. Look, I've been through all this.' She picked up Freeman's letter-opener, a small silver stiletto, and studied it, her crimson nails like gouts of blood upon its glittering surface.

'I know. We're about to go through it again.' He looked at her grimly and drew the first flash of anger from those small brown eyes. Then she took a deep breath and sighed heavily, measuring out her ennui in her respiration.

'I was at home, all evening. End of story.' She eased her chair back, stretched nylon-clad legs before her so that both she and her interrogators could study them the better.

'Witnesses?' intoned Bert Hook impassively. Lambert was not sure whether he was supporting his chief or breaking the spell of those shapely extensions.

'My mother. As you already know very well. That's all.' She folded her arms, swung the swivel chair a little, and stared at the ceiling. It was a caricature of the young executive at home in these surroundings; Lambert thought suddenly of Simon Hapgood. The difference was that Jane Davidson's pose drew attention to her high, firm breasts, which her movement strained against the thin lemon cotton of her blouse. Bert Hook met this interesting profile when he looked up from his note-taking. Lambert, who was determined to offer no smiles, carefully avoided his sergeant's face.

He said, 'Your neighbour saw you come in. She could not be sure whether you went out again or not. 'He was turning the notion on its head, but she was quick enough to spot it.

'You mean she didn't see me go out. That's because I didn't. Old Ma Bellingham doesn't miss much. Nosy old cow.'

'So your mother is your only witness?'

'So my mother's a liar? So how many witnesses have you got who saw me anywhere else?' The woman knew her rights. Perhaps she had been over the strengths of her story many times before in her own mind; perhaps, he thought ruefully, she merely realized that he could not trap her because she was telling the truth.

She reached languidly for her bag, placed it on her lap, extracted from its depths a packet of tipped cigarettes. She neither offered the packet to them nor asked if they objected to her smoking. She found a butane lighter, gazed full into Lambert's eyes as she lit the cigarette, and blew the first cloud of smoke gently into the air between them. Lambert had given up cigarettes two years ago and lately at Christine's insistence very nearly relinquished his pipe. The familiar sharp smell in his nostrils was a small torture, made more acute by the fancy that the girl knew exactly the stress she was imposing.

In another place, he might have dashed the

cigarette from her fingers and bidden her harshly not to smoke. But she had been charged with no offence. In the hoary but convenient phrase, she was helping police with their inquiries. Voluntarily, as a good citizen should. In the respectable working-class world where John Lambert had been brought up in the postwar years, young ladies did not paint their nails, and still less did they smoke. Since then, he had questioned a thousand sluts and whores and worse, quickly building a thick skin and a protective detachment. Now he found the prejudices ingrained in childhood as difficult for a grizzled policeman to discard as for others. He would have been surprised but scarcely gratified to find that placid Bert Hook would also like to have spanked this girl: the pleasure involved in the fantasy could scarcely be reconciled with CID objectivity.

'How did you get the job at Freeman Estates?' said Lambert. It was only pique that made him frame the question like that. Had he not been nettled by her appearance and bearing, he would merely have taken her through her time with the firm, trying to build up a picture of relatidnships with colleagues. As it was, he made it sound as if she could not have got the post merely on her merits. It was a departure from his own rules. And paradoxically, it struck home.

'Why shouldn't I have it? I'm good at it,' she almost shouted. The brown eyes, half shut with contempt for most of their initial exchange, were wide now with alarm.

It was Lambert's turn to be deliberately unhurried. He sorted through the papers in the file on the desk in front of him until he came to the photocopy of her application for the post. He glanced from her neat, small handwriting to the drawn face a few feet in front of him, dwelling on what he read, accentuating its significance in the sure knowledge that she would not recall exactly what she had set down here years earlier.

'You came here with very few qualifications. English Language and one other O-level.'

'I didn't work at school,' she muttered, flashing him a look of hate.

'No doubt. That doesn't explain why an employer would reward your indolence.' He was aware of Hook watching him: this wasn't at all his usual style. How far it was professional scenting of a weakness, how far a personal spite against a young woman who had got under his skin, he could not be sure himself. But he had opened a breach in her defences and he was driving through it as vigorously as he could, aware of his excitement but not his motive.

'I took a course.' She was almost a sullen schoolgirl as the shell of sophistication cracked around her. She still had her handbag on her knees, but now her fingers twisted and untwisted through the handle.

'Correction. You began a course. A secretarial course at the College of Further Education. Shorthand, Typewriting, Office Practice; all of which might have been valuable at Freeman Estates. Except that you only lasted a month on the course.'

'I got the chance of a job.'

'Really!' The cynicism as his lips curled the word was like a slap across the face. He did not like himself much, but he knew he was through the shell to the soft, unguarded interior. He thought of DI Rushton's words, 'We didn't turn up any motive, but both she and her mother seemed scared. We felt they were hiding something, but we couldn't find out what.'

He said quietly, 'Strange that in the middle of a recession as we were then, you should get a job here with minimal qualifications, while girls with six O-levels remained unemployed. Perhaps we'd better talk to your mother: she might be more cooperative.' Again there was that look of fear on the face that had lately been so hard and confident.

'What do you want to know?' she said wretchedly. She sat bolt upright now, the calves she had recently displayed so boldly tucked back under her seat, her shoulders hunched forward, as though to minimize the effect of the breasts she had shown to such advantage. Lambert remembered that she had no father, that she lived alone with a mother she helped to support. He should have hated his job, but the sense of a small triumph was stronger. If he softened his attitude, it was merely another tactic.

'All I'm anxious to do is to get as full a picture as possible of what goes on at Freeman Estates. Of what went on before the cold-blooded murder of your principal.' A small shiver shook the humped shoulders at his last phrase, but she did not look up at him. 'I need to know about your relationships with the other members of the firm. What about Simon Hapgood?'

She looked up at him in surprise. 'What about him?' She seemed for a moment puzzled but relieved, as if she had expected his questioning to take a different tack. 'I went out with him once or twice. If he can't get his hand straight up your skirt, he's not interested. He didn't get up mine. He's not concerned with me.'

'Then who?' said Lambert gently.

'Don't know. Not interested,' she said, just too quickly. Her mouth set in the sullen pout of childhood, and he realized he would get nothing further here. She looked close to exhaustion; he saw now how much of a pretence her earlier attitude had involved. She must have been dreading this further probing into what Rushton and his DCs had failed to discover. He recalled his wife's view that Jane Davidson was 'a good girl when you get through to her' and wondered how long ago she had formed that view. He had been pressing hard on a girl from what the social workers would call 'a deprived background'. Well, it was an unfortunate fact of police life that many serious criminals came from 'deprived backgrounds'.

'What about George Robson?' he asked after a pause. She relaxed a little further, attempted to smile. 'Mr Robson is all right. Randy old bugger, but a gentleman!' Apparently she did not consider this a paradox: Lambert decided he liked her for that. 'The firm is going to be a lot happier place, now he's in here.' She looked round approvingly at the trappings of office, the big mahogany desk, the internal and external telephones, the blotting-pad and desk inkstand that was never used. 'Miss Godson won't be able to order me about like dirt now,' she said with satisfaction.

'How did Miss Godson get on with Mr Freeman?' asked Lambert innocently.

'She hated him,' the girl said, promptly and with relish: she plainly felt she owed the firm's other woman no favours.

'Enough to kill him?' said Lambert. 'That's what Sergeant Hook and I are interested in.'

Jane Davidson showed shock, then the beginnings of a delicious excitement at the notion. She wiped her cheek with a tiny flowered handkerchief, then looked down at the smeared eye-shadow. Then she said reluctantly, 'No. Freeman had done something to hurt her, I'm sure, but I don't know what. But old Emily wouldn't kill him. She wouldn't have the bottle.'

' "Bottle" is a difficult thing to estimate, Jane,' said Lambert, reflecting that 'old Emily' was probably several years his junior. It was the first time he had used the receptionist's Christian name; perhaps now, with pretence stripped away, she was reminding him of his own laughter. 'All kinds of people acquire courage for a little while when they are desperate enough.' She nodded thoughtfully, stubbing out the last of the cigarette she had long forgotten in the big glass ashtray.

Lambert put aside his file on Jane Davidson and looked hard at her. 'Do you know of a man called Wino Willy?' he said.

Her eyes as she looked at him were full of strong emotions. He thought he caught fear and anger; then her face relaxed into an unexpected tenderness. Her voice very quiet, she said, 'I knew him as Mr Harrison. He was always very kind to me.'

'I believe you knew his son quite well at one time.'

Now there was a fierce pride as she said, 'Andrew. Yes, we were very close. He was a bit older than me but we got on well. I think perhaps if he hadn't—' She couldn't finish. If Lambert hadn't had years of experience, he

230

would have been tempted to reach out to the small white hand which clenched itself into a fist and pressed itself against her thigh.

Instead, he said gently, 'Do you still see Mr Harrison?'

She took a long time to reply, as if she were coming to a decision. 'Just occasionally,' she said. 'It used to be more often, but I think I only upset him. As a matter of fact, I saw him on the night before the murder.'

Another of his suspects in touch with the enigmatic figure on the moor just before the murder: Lambert scarcely knew whether he was elated or not. He had a feeling that the increased complexity, the extra dimension which he was adding to the killing of Stanley Freeman, would eventually point the solution, but as yet he could not see how. He said lamely, 'How did he seem?'

She looked at him in surprise. 'As usual, I suppose. I took a friend's dog which had an infected paw. He bound it up with some herbs against the wound. While he was concentrating on that, he seemed quite normal. Like a mother with her baby.' Perhaps she surprised herself with the simile, for she stopped and seemed near to tears again at the recollection. 'As soon as he'd finished, he danced away from me as wild as ever. I couldn't get through to him; I might have been a total stranger.'

Lambert, who had for a few moments on the moor felt himself in touch with that ravaged mind, caught something of the tragedy she felt in her last phrase. Well, at least the dog would make it easy to verify the facts of her story. It might of course have been a carefully chosen excuse to visit Willy: their former relationship suggested Jane would have a closer contact than almost anyone with the man who was now Wino Willy.

She was relaxed now, nervously drained but relieved by the thought that her ordeal was almost over. It was a good moment to play a trump card in this strange game which was the staple diet of detection. Lambert's voice was carefully even as he said, 'And what about your own relationship with Stanley Freeman?'

He watched the scarlet nails fasten on the butt of the cigarette she had already discarded, then grind it on and on, until it was dry shreds in the glass bowl. Her voice when it came was dry-throated and low, as if it belonged to a much older woman. All she said was, 'I didn't like him,' but the croaking delivery shocked all three of them.

'Did you kill him?' Lambert was still as a snake. The brown eyes widened with fear, sunk in hollows which seemed darker in the young face.

'No. I could never have killed him.' The voice was so low they had to strain to hear it. Faintly through the thick walls, they caught the sound of the telephone in the outer office, which Jane Davidson would normally have answered. Emily Godson, who had taken over her duties for the duration of this interview, must have answered it, but they caught nothing of her voice.

'What car do you drive, Miss Davidson?' said Lambert quietly.

'A white Fiesta.'

'A company car?' Lambert, who knew the answers here, was checking her reactions.

'Yes. Part of the pool, in case anyone is objecting.' She was watching him warily, trying to find where this led and who had objected to her possession of the car. But she did not look threatened.

He switched directly back to her relationship with the dead man. 'It was quite clear earlier that there was something odd about your original appointment here.' She nodded dumbly, signifying her acquiescence now, not trusting herself to speak. 'I have to advise you that your best policy if you are not involved in this murder is to be perfectly frank with us. The innocent have nothing to fear; any confidences which have nothing to do with the case will be respected.' He went on with the soothing phrases, pouring them like medication over the hunched figure opposite him.

Jane Davidson sat with her handbag pressed against her like a shield, the handkerchief clutched in one of the small white fists as the tears ran unheeded down her face. She looked at the edge of the desk in front of her, not at the two men who had brought her to this disclosure.

Then she said dully, 'Stanley Freeman was my father.'

CHAPTER TWENTY-TWO

Wino Willy watched the green woodpecker.

It came nearer, its sharp brown eye fixed unblinkingly on the man it had known for months. And Willy, so tremulous in any human arena, sat quiet as stone. The bird hopped between Willy's large feet, removed the ants with tongue swifter than a striking snake's, and looked up into the lined face above him. Willy looked back at the bird and said nothing, though his throat purred a scarcely audible welcome. The sleek crimson head investigated his right boot in detail, found it wanting, and looked to the tall oaks and the sky beyond them. The bird hopped unhurriedly away, then rose and wheeled in undulating flight into the wood. Willy heard its call like derisive laughter behind him.

His mind was deciding for the first time in years upon a plan of action. For a long time he had moved as instinctively and thoughtlessly as the wild creatures around him, his course motivated by the same needs of food and shelter that they felt. But not as freely as them: he was a man still. Weighed down now by a burden he had thought to have escaped from for ever, he wrestled with what he had once called conscience. A notion unknown to birds and beasts.

He knew now that he should have restricted himself to those birds and beasts, for human contact was not to be trusted. This human had brought him food and drink and proposed a monster jape. He remembered the very phrase: like Billy Bunter and those boys who had never existed. But it was not a jape, and now that it had gone wrong he must tell. When he had gone down to the house and told the woman this morning, she had yelled at him to be quiet and fled from him. He could hear her screams still; they had rung in his ears long after he had come away.

But he would tell the man who had come to him on the moor. He would put it right. That man knew what a piece of work is man. ' "How noble in reason! how infinite in faculty! in action how like an angel!" ' Willy found himself tossing the ironic phrases to the empty sky, while the green woodpecker mocked his inaction from the shadowy depths behind him. And in that moment he knew what he must do.

He had thought to wait until the man came to him again on the moor. But that might take days, and in that time . . .

Willy stood, grew tall, buttoned his ragged

coat. It was not cold, but he was gathering his resources and his resolution about him. Only he knew the courage this was taking him, though Lambert would later divine it. For Wino Willy was going back by his own resolution into the world of men. Of buildings, crowded with the humanity that scared him more than bombs. Of sniggers, and sly smiles, and assurances that could not be trusted. Of japes that led to death. He kicked the tree-stump he had sat on, feeling the pain on his instep as a reassurance of the reality of his humanity. Then he set off, before his resolution could fail.

And so while Lambert questioned the associates of Stanley Freeman, the man who knew his murderer moved towards him. He kept to the common as long as he could, working his way parallel to the straggling hawthorn hedge which marked its boundary. He chattered to the blackbirds and thrushes which sang around him, scolded the pair of magpies which sailed in like aircraft from the field below. His tall, tatterdemalion figure looked like a modern Pied Piper against the skyline as he whistled and chattered his way along, but no birds or mammals followed his erratic course as he moved towards the world of men. He did not see the human eyes that watched him from the road beyond the hedge.

The common was his territory. He knew every clump of prickly gorse, every tiny knoll of ground, each of the three peaty hollows where black water lurked to soak the unwary. He could move surefootedly across here, even on moonless nights, as occasionally he did when dark visions and darker memories made sleep impossible. He was frightened, but determined now; the excitement rose like a drug to give him courage. The spires and roofs of Oldford came into view. He was doing the right thing. It was a sensation he had not known for years and his flesh prickled at it.

He was nearly at the point where he would have to join the road. As he approached it, a black and white collie-type dog came joyfully to meet him. It escaped regularly from the council estate to join Willy in his free world of common and moor; they greeted each other as old friends.

The hawthorn here was in luxuriant summer growth. Any day now, the council lorry with its flail cutter would bring its swift, harsh discipline to the road side of the hedge, even in this scarcely used lane, but the common side would remain untouched. Willy walked quickly behind the dog, prodigal with his energy to prevent his heart from quailing.

He took in almost everything, with darting glances which dwelt on no single object: not the wild flowers at the base of the hedge, nor the fast-moving banks of cloud that suddenly obscured the sun, nor even the horses in the field on the other side of the lane. Almost everything: he did not notice the car, rolling silently in neutral down the long slope behind him. The eyes followed him steadily wherever the gaps in the hawthorn allowed; the person whose fingers moved so delicately upon the steering-wheel had guessed now where Willy was going. And what he was about.

The lane was not wide where Willy joined it. The growth of the hedges meant that there was no room for pedestrians to the side of the tarmac surface. Willy chanted instructions to the happy, heedless dog which trotted beside him. 'Always face approaching traffic,' he said. 'Keep your head up and your shoulders back and swing your arms.' He was quoting his father forty years ago: it suddenly seemed much closer than that. A small red van did indeed come towards them, passing man and dog as they slowed, the driver waving a cheerful acknowledgement of their caution.

Willy gave the dog's head a swift stroke, then strode boldly forward and quoted his father again. 'Put some swank into it!' he said. He swung his arms extravagantly high, up above his waist, until eventually he marched like a swift tin soldier and his hands swung as high as his shoulders, as he had seen his dead son's hands swing as he watched him long ago through the railings of the school playground. He sang and he giggled. And the little dog laughed to see such fun.

He never even heard the car behind him. It

came up with him where the road dropped narrow and steep between the high hedges. The dog's acute ears caught the noise of its harsh acceleration and leapt sideways beneath the hedge, but Willy was singing too boisterously to catch the warning. He moved automatically sideways after the dog, lost his balance, made it easy for the ruthless driver.

He fell beneath the wheels as they leapt forward, his legs smashed like sticks beneath the offside ones, his head ground sickeningly on the edge of the road within a yard of the terrified dog. His last thought was of his dead son, his last sensation as he entered the darkness one of a vast relief.

The driver checked the front of the car before looking at the body. Wino Willy Harrison had been accommodating to the last. Falling beneath the wheels, he had not even damaged the front fender. Only the tyres had touched him. A brisk dash through the ford where this old lane neared the village would remove almost all trace of the episode. The driver did not need to approach too close to Willy's shattered corpse to be sure that he could speak no more. The dog whined hopelessly for a moment beside the spatter of blood and brain upon the grass, then slunk through the hedge and was gone.

As the first heavy drops of rain began to fall, the car moved swiftly away.

CHAPTER TWENTY-THREE

In the office of Freeman Estates, Superintendent and Sergeant sat looking at each other and feeling rather stupid.

Jane Davidson had been released to the limited comforts of the washroom, but Bert Hook was still bewildered by her melodramatic revelation. Even Lambert, who had trained himself over twenty years to be surprised by nothing, had to admit that it had not been what he expected.

'Do you believe her?' said Hook.

'Yes, I think so. We'll check it out, of course, but she's no fool, our Miss Davidson, despite her school career. She knows we'll check. And it fits the facts. It answers the questions about how she got the job and a car the others thought she didn't warrant, and what it was that both she and her mother were concealing.'

'Does it remove her from our list of suspects?' Bert Hook, whose conjectures about what Miss Davidson had been hiding had run on other, more conventional, lines, was too shaken to think clearly yet. Or perhaps he had dropped into the flattering but unhelpful habit of letting his superintendent lead his thinking.

'You know better than that, Bert. Over half of homicides are domestic. A high proportion of them are children killing fathers because of real or imagined grievances.'

'But usually on impulse.' Bert Hook was chauvinist enough to reject the vision of a young girl clenching her father's drunken wrists in a grip of iron as he struggled to remove the plastic bag which was asphyxiating him.

'Agreed. But the Jane Davidson she chose to present to us in the first part of our interview would be quite capable of planning and executing this kind of killing, once she was convinced of its justice. Where do the Davidsons live?'

'On the council estate.'

'We'll have to question Jane's mother, but all the signs are that the eminent Mr Freeman neither acknowledged his daughter nor made financial provision for her mother. That seems like par for the course for him.' He was thinking of Margot Jones and the life left to her. And his golfing metaphor was not accidental: he longed to be out of this claustrophobic office and the increasingly sordid Freeman Estates, breathing the clear air of his golf course and walking quietly between high trees.

'Stanley Freeman has left a wife who is scarcely grieving and four employees who are glad he's gone. The more I find out about him, the less I regret his passing. But no one's going to get away with murder if we can help it.' It sounded in his ears like a slogan, the kind of thing naïve young inspectors offered to hungry pressmen. 'Sorry, Bert, I need to lash myself into action from time to time.'

'At least one of these five is lying,' said Hook, feeling the need of a truism himself to focus the discussion.

'Probably two or three. Maybe all five. The problem is to distinguish the lies which connect with the murder from those people tell to protect their own secrets.' Lambert shuffled his papers on the late Stanley Freeman's big desk and prepared rather wearily to be objective. 'Emily Godson and Jane Davidson have given us accounts of their movements on the night of the murder, which we may suspect but have not so far disproved. Emily says she was with nutty Aunt Alice, Jane with her mother. Negative evidence supports their stories, in that we have not unearthed anyone who saw either of them, or their cars, anywhere else on that Wednesday night. Let's put them aside for the moment. What about the others?'

Hook turned the pages of his notebook ponderously, indulging a mannerism: he knew well enough the facts he wanted, without referring to its contents. 'George Robson was seen by three different people with his dog on the common in the important hour between eight and nine. He's the only one who seems to be in the clear, thanks to Fred and his walks. I like Fred,' said Bert Hook inconsequentially.

Lambert saw the golden labrador with his body across the Sergeant's feet and his soft head in Bert's large, friendly hands. The tadpole of an idea wriggled in the recesses of his mind, swam briefly, and disappeared again into the darkness. 'What car does Robson drive?'

'A red Sierra Ghia,' said Hook instantly, too practised to be thrown by the apparent *non sequiturs* of his chief.

'Which leads us,' said Lambert, jumping a couple of sentences like an old married man in conversation with his wife, 'to Simon Hapgood. Still no definite corroboration of when he arrived in the pub that night?'

'Nothing definite. More sightings: none certain before nine o'clock. He seems to have been boisterous to draw attention to himself, and anxious to give the impression he'd been there for hours to anyone who met him.' Hook wondered if he was being fair: he disliked the blond and extrovert Mr Hapgood, though he did not care to analyse his distaste in case it owed something to jealousy. But then his chief had always encouraged him to air his prejudices freely in these confidential exchanges. So he was quite bold in pointing out, 'He drives a blue Sierra.'

'Sergeant Hook, you sound quite smug about it. Nothing more definite from the Harbens about the blue car they saw, is there?'

'No. They've been shown a brochure picture of a blue Sierra, but they couldn't be sure. They saw the car against the low evening sun, and they were busy taking evading action. "A medium-sized dark blue car" is as far as they can go. Hapgood is the only one of our suspects with a blue car.'

Lambert spent thirty seconds in deep, frowning thought. Then he said, 'For what it's worth, which at this moment is precisely nothing, I don't believe Mr Hapgood's story. Let's have him in again. He should be back here shortly. Meantime, what do you think of the grieving widow, beyond the fact that black suits her and she knows it?'

Bert Hook started a little guiltily from his picture of Denise Freeman at the graveside. She had worn her mourning like an elegant uniform, and uniforms on women always turned him on; even stolid sergeants were allowed their not-so-innocent fantasies.

'What did she stand to gain?' he said, daring to answer a superintendent with a question of his own.

Lambert shrugged. 'Freedom, Bert. She'd had enough of the contemptible Stanley. She doesn't get the business, but she gets a salary from it, and everything else. Plus her freedom to live how she wants. And with whom she wants, perhaps.'

Silence. They indulged their own thoughts about the chic Mrs Freeman. Eventually,

Lambert speculated on whether these pauses were longer in the case of attractive females than corpulent men. Then he told himself he must beware of this philosophic vein.

'She drives a green Volvo,' said Bert Hook.

'Which might be mistaken for blue against the evening sun. I saw it. And no one seems to have seen it in the car park at Tewkesbury. Nor did anyone notice the scarcely anonymous Denise in or around the cinema.'

'I think she's lying,' said Hook. It sounded like sycophancy, a mere attempt to follow his superior's thinking and anticipate its conclusion. In fact, he had just made up his own mind, and was surprised to hear himself voicing his thoughts almost as they formed.

Lambert looked at him with a quick little smile: sometimes there was still something very boyish in his sergeant. 'So do I. What puzzles me is that I think if she'd planned to murder her husband, she'd have organized something much better than a visit to the cinema as an alibi. Compared with the thought that went into the murder itself, it all seems rather improvised.'

Suddenly, the middle of the three phones in front of him bleeped, loud as a trapped bird in the quiet room. Lambert picked it up automatically: he had left the number with the murder room. Rushton's voice was urgent. Lambert made him wait while Hook went to the door and opened it a fraction to check that

245

Emily Godson was not listening at the reception desk, where she still sat. She was not: so there was a direct outside line from Freeman's office. A fact which held its own interest.

'Go ahead,' said Lambert to his Inspector.

'Denise Freeeman, sir. We've come up with a sighting of her in Tewkesbury.'

'Where?'

'In the cinema. At the interval. She was sitting where she said, in the circle.'

'Reliable?'

'Oh, I think so, sir. It's a distant friend of Mrs Freeman's. She was sitting on the other side of the cinema, so she didn't speak to her, but she saw her when the lights were up, both before the main film and immediately after it.'

Lambert flirted with the idea of a distant friend being brought in by Denise Freeman to support her story, but found it unlikely.

Rushton had saved his real news for last, treasuring his titbit as long as possible. He said, trying ineffectively to conceal his satisfaction, 'There's just one thing wrong with it, sir. This wasn't on the Wednesday night when the murder was committed. It was on the previous Monday.'

CHAPTER TWENTY-FOUR

Simon Hapgood was in earnest, low-toned conversation with Jane Davidson at the reception desk. Bert Hook's size elevens approached noiselessly to within eight feet before the Sergeant's voice, investing the innocent words with quiet menace, said, 'The Superintendent would like a few words with you now, Mr Hapgood.'

Backs, Hook decided, could be more revealing than he had ever allowed. He watched Hapgood's shoulders rise in tension beneath the immaculately cut gold hair. When the man turned with broad, toothpaste smile, the Sergeant knew how much effort had gone into forming the lips into this caricature of relaxation. And when Hapgood twirled his car keys on his fingers and said, 'By all means, Officer,' Hook thought that from close range he could detect fear in the cold blue eyes.

It was still there a moment later, when Hapgood looked at the Superintendent across the mahogany desk of his dead employer. Lambert was buoyant. The case had begun to move; his mind grew sharper with the thought. With confidence came an irritation with the pretensions and the deceptions of Simon Hapgood. It was time this dubious young man learned not to take on the big battalions.

He said without preamble, 'I won't waste time. Further information has come to light.' About Jane Davidson and Denise Freeman, not you, but you don't know that. So start squirming. 'I advise you to think carefully. Have you anything to add to your statement about your movements on the night of Stanley Freeman's murder?'

Hapgood licked dry lips and tried to think. Thoughts came, but they were the thoughts of a mind in panic; incoherent, disorganized, leading to no useful conclusion. He forced a smile, swallowed, said, 'I don't think so. I came home, had a light meal—'

'We are familiar with your account, there is no need to repeat it,' said Lambert, eyes relentlessly on the callow face. The renewed catalogue of Hapgood's movements might bring a calm he was not going to allow. 'I ask you again, do you wish to make any variation in that story?'

'No.' The blue eyes looked not at his tormentor but past him, over his shoulder, to the framed certificates on the wall beyond the drinks cabinet. Lambert was suddenly reminded of a Luftwaffe pilot, with blond hair and empty blue eyes above blue uniform. As a very small boy, he had seen such a man led from his crashed plane, dazed and fearful; he did not know whether this image was a memory of that moment or of the myriad layers of film and television which now

248

overlaid it. Nor could he have said how far it affected his attitude to Hapgood at this point. His next move determined the course of the interview.

'Mr Hapgood, you were not in the Stonemasons' Arms at eight o'clock, as you claim. You were seen there all right, by numerous witnesses: all after nine p.m.'

'I was there earlier than that. On my own. The pub doesn't fill up until quite late on Wednesdays.'

Lambert let him go on until his words petered out. Each phrase came with less conviction, until the voice died almost to a whine. Hapgood rearranged the red tie on the brilliant white shirt, tried to find the end of it of absorbing interest, found his eyes drawn back inexorably to the Superintendent's sphinxlike face. Lambert, more certain now than if he had concrete evidence in his hands, closed his trap. He could see himself from without, like an actor speaking someone else's lines, utterly confident of the outcome because Hapgood's responses too were now fixed.

'You arrived at the Stonemasons' Arms and parked your blue Sierra at just about nine p.m. You entered through the outside toilets, arriving in the pub as if you were in fact returning from there.' It was an old trick of petty crooks in city pubs, in his days as a detective-constable twenty years and more ago.

Hapgood was only a petty crook in executive's clothing. He swallowed twice before he could speak, the blood draining from his fresh, unlined face until it looked like parchment. In a strange, old man's voice, he said, 'I—I didn't kill Freeman.'

There was a long pause, the detectives, in no hurry now, waited for him to elaborate. Perhaps, if he could have trusted his voice, he would have done so. Perhaps the habits of deceit he had lived by prevented a willing disclosure of the truth, even when, like them, he realized it was now inevitable.

Hook glanced at his chief, received an assent that would have been invisible to those outside their circle, and said harshly, 'You're going to have to convince us of that. Having lied to the police for over a week, you'll have to work hard.'

The pale blue eyes looked from one unyielding face to the other in front of him. Then, as the handsome head nodded a hopeless acknowledgement, the gaze fell to the carpet between the Italian leather shoes. Hapgood's mouth had become a thin white slit; still he did not speak.

Lambert switched instinctively from stick to carrot in an effort to keep his man's tongue moving while his mind reeled. 'You may smoke if you like. While you do, I should consider your position.' In the ambience they had created, this perfectly sound advice became a threat.

Hapgood produced packet and lighter, selected a cigarette, lit it at the second attempt. He watched his hands with a fascination that was almost comic, as if they belonged to someone else. Belatedly, he remembered his audience, offered the packet, and received two solemn refusals. His movements were almost in slow motion, as he strove for the relaxation which would not come. Eventually he succeeded in lighting his cigarette, then watched the flame of the lighter for a moment. In the heavy silence, they caught the note of Jane Davidson's voice from the switchboard, the tone cheerful, emollient, efficient as she dealt with a caller. It seemed to come from another and more innocent world.

'You aren't the only one to lie about your movements,' said Lambert eventually, probing for a reaction, suggesting as he had done throughout that he knew more than he did.

Hapgood shot him a quick, wary glance. It was the look of a cornered animal, but there was no defiance left in him. He said, 'She didn't kill Freeman either.' He presumed his tormentors knew who the 'she' was; he took a long, nervous draw on his cigarette.

And suddenly Lambert did know. Once he had accepted the idea, it seemed so obvious he felt a fool for not considering it much earlier. Hook's quick glance of surprise was small consolation as he said, 'You might care to know that Mrs Freeman's account of her movements on that Wednesday night has already been discredited. We now know that she was at the cinema in Tewkesbury not on that night, as she claimed, but on the previous Monday.'

Hapgood nodded: it was only what he had expected to hear. 'We were together on that Wednesday night.' Then, as if to avoid further questions, he said, 'Between seven o'clock and ten to nine.' This precision could only mean that he had thought about the times and their significance on many occasions in the preceding days. Probably he realized this, for his face relaxed into a grisly smile as he studied the grey smoke rising slowly from the end of his cigarette.

'During which time you executed the murder of Stanley Freeman,' said Lambert. He made it sound as matter-of-fact as an item of shopping. Perhaps his tone misled Simon Hapgood, for it took him two long seconds to react.

Then he shouted, 'No! No, we didn't!' at a level which must have carried throughout the building. Lambert, watching his victim intently, still had time to wonder what the reactions of Emily Godson and Jane Davidson must be beyond the heavy door; George Robson was still out. 'You can't think that,' said Hapgood; his voice was lower this time, but the edge of

252

panic belied his words. Hook, a man not given to fanciful conceits, thought he could smell fear on the man.

Lambert turned the screw. 'This is a murder inquiry, Mr Hapgood. Both you and Mrs Freeman have impeded it by premeditated deceit over several days. It is not unreasonable for us to assume that you are guilty of conspiring to murder Mrs Freeman's husband. The onus at this moment is on you to convince us otherwise.'

It was not true, of course. Morally he might be right, but the law would not support him. As if to rebuke him, Hapgood now said dully, 'I want to speak to my solicitor before this goes any further.' It was the dull note of despair: he had taken the Superintendent's words at their face value. But his face showed that he might yet be led where they wanted.

Lambert said, 'That is your right of course at any time. But we have made no charges yet. You are merely helping the police with their inquiries.' It attempted to get the best of both worlds, raising a brief hope in Hapgood, then reminding him with the familiar official jargon of the seriousness of his position.

And it worked. Hapgood looked from one to the other and said wearily, 'What do you want to know?'

At a nod from his chief, Hook moved in to play the hard man. He opened his notebook portentously and said, 'You should give us a

253

detailed account of what you now say you did between seven and nine on the night of the murder.' The phrasing was not lost on the discomforted Senior Negotiator. For a revealing moment, he looked at the sergeant with hatred, but Hook, with pen poised, stared down at his blank page with impassive distaste.

'I was with Denise, that's all,' said Hapgood sullenly.

'Where?' said Hook.

'At her place. In bed, for God's sake!' Hapgood glanced at Lambert, found no relief in the Superintendent's steady examination of his face, and looked down at his feet. He plucked an imaginary hair from where no hair lay on the knee of his trousers. His face looked thinner for his ordeal; the immaculate blue suit seemed now a fraction too large for the body which carried it.

'Were you there throughout this period on that Wednesday evening?' Hook somehow managed to incorporate scepticism into his delivery of the cumbrous phrasing.

'Yes.'

'Have you witnesses?'

'Oh, for goodness' sake!' Hapgood could not bring off the attempt at indignation. He declined into a resentful monotone. 'We were in bed together for most of the time. Do you expect witnesses to that?'

Hook, who chose to treat the question as rhetorical, wrote carefully and controlled his imagination.

It was Lambert who said, 'Sergeant Hook is inviting you to help yourself. You have until this evening lied steadily to us about your actions on the night of the murder. You are now asking us to believe that you were in bed throughout the vital hour with the wife of the victim.'

'It's true! Ask Denise.'

'Oh, we shall, Mr Hapgood. But you're now saying that the only witness to your new story is the wife of the deceased. A woman who has lied comprehensively about her actions on that evening. Who on her own admission was at odds with her husband, who was killed at the time when the two of you claim to have been alone together.'

'Why do you think we killed him?' There was horror in the young eyes, but whether the horror of a murderer discovered or an innocent accused it was impossible to say. Hapgood was thirty, but he looked as if he was completing the business of growing up only with the present crisis.

Lambert did not trouble himself with any cautious disclaimer. 'Look at it from our point of view, Mr Hapgood. A man is carrying on an affair with a woman who is ready to be rid of her husband. That husband is murdered, by a preconceived and meticulously executed method. Both the wife and her lover lie about their actions on the evening of the death.

When those lies are exposed, they admit they were together for that evening. Unobserved by anyone. It's a classic scenario for murder, with a classic motive. Young man persuaded to the deed by infatuation with an older woman. You might even be able to persuade a jury you were an inexperienced lad who was led out of his depth, but I wouldn't count on it.'

'It wasn't like that.' Hapgood had a hopeless air about him now, as if he were already in a cell.

Lambert let him dwell upon his situation for a moment, without ever ceasing to study him. Then he said, 'If it wasn't you, you will need someone other than Denise Freeman to support your story. You went to her bungalow in your own car, presumably?'

'Yes.' Hapgood nodded to support the scarcely audible word.

'And you parked it in the drive there?'

'No. I left it at the end of the lane. I always did. It seemed more discreet.' In the face of murder, the small deceits of adultery seemed insignificant now, and he smiled bleakly, apologetically.

'How long had your affair with Mrs Freeman been going on?'

'Six months.' He had no need to hesitate here: it was a computation he had made for his own purposes on the morning after the death of Freeman.

'How many people know about it?'

256

'None, that I know of. I told you. We were discreet; neither of us wanted it broadcast.'

It was the usual way. Lovers were always sanguine about their security. The husband might be the last to know, but other people usually discovered relationships fairly quickly: lovers always underestimate the curiosity of the uninvolved. On the other hand, Denise Freeman was a cool and competent planner, who had no doubt undertaken this sort of thing before. She would organize secrecy better than most.

'What about the people who worked with you?'

'They didn't know.'

'You can't assume that because they didn't mention it to you. They're in a position to know more than anyone else about your movements, because of the appointments you have with clients.'

He shrugged. 'If they'd known about it, they'd have let me know they knew. They didn't.' It was a shrewd enough assessment: no doubt he had considered it long before the murder. If either Emily Godson or Jane Davidson had known about it, wouldn't they have used it to taunt or threaten him? Neither of them was fond of Hapgood, to say the least. Unless, of course, they planned to use the information to incriminate him in a murder inquiry. Lambert remembered Jane Davidson saying dismissively of Hapgood, 'He's not concerned with me,' then denying too quickly any knowledge of his commitments elsewhere.

'Someone may have seen your car on that Wednesday night.'

Hapgood said dully, 'It's a blue Ford Sierra. Registration number—'

'We have the number. Where exactly was it parked?'

'Near the end of Orchard Lane, where Denise lives. There's a five-barred gate leading into a field, where it's possible to park a car off the road. I usually leave it there.'

Scarcely invisible. Only lovers, with hormones beating an urgent tattoo, would consider this discreet. Now imprudence might work in their favour: someone might have seen the vehicle in the vital hour. If it had really been there. More tedious leg-work for DC and the local uniformed man. Meanwhile, he would see Denise Freeman and shatter that air of Gallic superiority. No doubt her new account of her movements would be close to Hapgood's, but he would probe it hard, turn it over and over to discover some discrepancy with her lover's version. A disparity that might send her for a long term in Holloway.

For the second time that day, his thoughts were disturbed by the shrill interruption of the telephone on the big desk. He felt Hapgood's wide, hypnotized eyes upon him as he picked it up, as if he had some premonition of calamity.

As he listened, Lambert's eyes turned

directly back to the man opposite him. He put the phone down, gathered his thoughts, and said quietly, 'Have you ever been to Lydon Hall in your car? Be careful: it's important.'

'Never.'

'Not even to photograph the place for your publicity material about it?'

Ironically, Hapgood thought it must be important to convince them. He said anxiously, 'No. Freeman did all that for Lydon Hall. What is this about?'

Lambert said heavily, 'I asked one of our detective-sergeants to take samples from the tyre-treads of all the firm's cars, with particular attention to yours, since a similar blue car was seen leaving the area of Lydon Hall immediately after the murder. These samples have now been tested against samples of gravel from the drive of Lydon Hall at our forensic laboratories.'

'With what results?' said Hapgood. He looked pale but composed—until Lambert answered him.

'I have to tell you that there were traces of gravel in your tyres identical with that of the Lydon Hall drive. Perhaps you had better ring that lawyer, Mr Hapgood.'

CHAPTER TWENTY-FIVE

The old road along the edge of the common was very little used. It was single track with passing places, and the ford where it left the town varied in depth with the seasons. Anyone in a hurry preferred the newer road along the bottom of the valley. The remains of Wino Willy lay undiscovered for some time.

When the cyclist dismounted reluctantly to examine the body, the sun was already low enough for the road to be in shadow here, where it ran between grassy banks and high stone walls. He saw the crushed head, retched his sensibilities into the ditch a few yards further on, and rode unsteadily down to the police station in Oldford with his news.

Half an hour later, the crew of the police control car examined the road, measured, looked for clues to give the detail of the accident. Decently anonymous in plastic and blanket, Willy's mortal remains were loaded into the ambulance. It moved away almost noiselessly down the hill, its blue light flashing eerily while its siren remained silent. There was no hurry now for Willy.

The police found little in their brief examination of the spot. The victim was a tramp and a 'wino', so no doubt it had been his own fault. There would be an end to female reportings of the wild man on the moor: one more minor irritant in their world had been removed. Nevertheless, people should report accidents, even when they were in no way to blame. A hit-and-run death would be an unwelcome statistic in their weekly records.

For a little while, no one in the uniformed branch at the station connected the death of Arthur James Harrison with the murder inquiry being conducted by CID in the terrapin behind the building. At six o'clock Sergeant Johnson came on to desk duty, noted the death of Wino Willy, and remembered the Superintendent's interest in the background of the dead man. At 6.14 he informed DI Rushton in the Murder Room of the death, and Willy was restored to his last, posthumous role in the investigation into the death of Stanley Freeman.

At that moment, Lambert was interviewing Denise Freeman. She admitted she had lied about her cinema visit, without being anything like as shaken as her lover had been. Yes, she had spent the evening with Hapgood, most of it in bed. He had left her at about 8.50, which tallied with his now admitted arrival at the Stonemasons' Arms at about nine. The precision of the detail convinced the Superintendent that she had already conferred with Hapgood about the new story. Whether it was the truth, or a new fabrication to conceal their dual guilt, it was impossible to tell from her bearing.

When Lambert asked why she had given them the false story about her movements on the night of the murder, she gave a Gallic shrug of those slim, attractive shoulders and said, 'I was not proud to be in bed with a man twelve years my junior on the night my husband was killed. I don't suppose Simon was proud either; anyway, his instinct is to conceal things.' There was just enough contempt in her voice for him to be convinced that the affair with Hapgood would not be continued. Then she went on, 'Perhaps in France there would be less embarrassment about such things, though we can be much more provincial than you in other ways. It was wrong of course to try to hide things: I should have known the efficiency of the English police would find me out.' The black eyes sparkled like newly split coal, the perfectly formed lips turned neither up nor down at the edges: it was impossible to tell whether even in the discovery of her falsehoods she was not mocking them a little.

Lambert wanted to shake her, to establish or to dismiss once and for all the notion of a lovers' pact to kill her husband. But he needed to get up on to the moor before dark, to find Wino Willy Harrison and discover what it was he had to tell. For the tadpole of an idea which had flicked its disturbing tail in his mind had become stronger, was swimming through murky, uncertain waters. Willy's evidence would kill it, or let it wax strong.

As he tried to hurry his questioning of the poised and puzzling Denise Freeman, the bleep of his car phone came faint but insistent from the drive outside her front door. Hook went out to answer it; he came back grim-faced, as his chief watched the widow's face intently during her answers. Superintendent and Sergeant went to the corner of the long lounge, still full of evening sun from its picture windows, and Hook recounted in low, sombre tones the incomplete details of the death of Wino Willy.

Denise Freeman watched them with Mona Lisa smile, as if she still found it impossible to take seriously the earnestness of these large men. When Lambert returned to her, she was shaken visibly for the first time in their exchanges: his voice was like a whiplash.

'Where were you this afternoon?'

'Here, most of the time. I went into Oldford to do a little shopping at about three-thirty.' She took her time over the reply, but her calm now required an effort they could observe.

'Witnesses?'

'None, here. My gardener left as usual at about one. In the town, the shopkeepers might remember me.' She mentioned the names of the greengrocery and bakery in Oldford; for the first time, she seemed anxious to establish her innocence. 'Oh, and I did see George Robson briefly, in the public car park.'

'Time?' As Hook noted her replies, Lambert rapped out his questions with an impatience that was nearly brutal.

'I—I couldn't be certain. It was when I arrived there. I should think about three forty-five. He was going back into the office. He could at least confirm that I was there at that time. Is it important?' For her, it was a note of weakness: it was the first time she had expressed any anxiety about her situation.

Lambert scarcely noticed. 'We'll need a statement from you, Mrs Freeman,' he said. Then he was away, leaving her disturbed and frustrated behind him, the engine of the big Vauxhall revving fiercely even as Hook scrambled hastily into the front passenger seat.

Usually, Lambert used his periods in the car to think, driving slowly, even at times lethargically, as his brain clicked forward. His subordinates even called him 'Super-gran' when he was driving, though they took care to keep it well out of his hearing. Tonight, he drove very fast; not dangerously, but with extreme concentration and not a word to his passenger. Hook was glad of his safety-belt, for the first time he could remember in this car.

Bert Hook, despite his comfortable contours, could move quickly when he had to. In his fast-bowling days, many an unwary batsman had been run out by underestimating his sprightly fielding. Tonight, he had great difficulty in keeping up with his superintendent without breaking into a run. As he strode across the common, Lambert's legs kept pace with his racing brain, the movement a physical release for his frustration.

For the tadpole of an idea had become a frog. An ugly frog, which leapt on swiftly from fact to fact in this case, finding a sure foothold each time, until it stared him unwinkingly in the face.

There were several people walking their dogs at this hour, but they quickly deferred to the urgency of the strange pair in suits and city shoes. It was fine again now, but the slight breeze was having a last fling before the inevitable calm of sundown. Fern and gorse danced in turn around them as they strode onwards and upwards, until they climbed the low stile that led from common to moor. Now they left the path, following steep rises beside the tiny tumbling stream that led like a white ribbon up towards the hidden sheepfold where Willy had made his sometime home.

'Couldn't Willy's death have been a straightforward road accident?' panted Hook, trailing in the wake of his chief and hoping to slow him by conversation.

'It was murder,' said Lambert bitterly. Murder which might have been prevented, had I only been available when Willy guessed the truth, he thought.

'You know who did it?'

'I know.' Even Lambert was blowing now,

forcing himself on like a Victorian trained in the dogma of cold baths and driving physical work-outs. He offered no more words, and Hoak was experienced enough not to press.

He watched Lambert's lean figure ahead of him, climbing without pause until he stopped, silhouetted against the evening sky, waiting until Hook arrived heavily alongside him. 'What are we up here for? Willy's in the mortuary,' said the long-suffering Sergeant, deciding that this time the pause was long enough for him to expend so much of his scanty resources of breath.

'Evidence,' said Lambert, briefly and abstractedly, as if impatient of one who needed to be informed of anything so obvious. He thrust out an arm across the chest of Hook, as if to prevent him plunging on enthusiastically down the small slope which dropped ahead of them before the next steady gradient: a most unlikely eventuality.

Then the Sergeant saw the object of Lambert's attention. Two hundred yards away, a golden labrador chased a carrion crow exuberantly across rough ground. When he was within five yards of it, the bird rose and flew heavily back over the dog's head, cawing contemptuously as it went. The dog gave it a ritual, good-natured bark, the farewell of a hunter who had never expected to catch his prey. Then he loped unhurriedly away from them, until he passed out of sight over the next rise.

The two observers looked at each other. 'Fred,' said Hook unnecessarily.

'"The little dog laughed, to see such fun . . ." Willy quoted that to us when we came up here to see him,' said Lambert. 'And he told us, "Every dog has its day." And his last words then were, "The more I see of men, the better I like dogs." If I'd made the connection earlier, poor Willy might be alive now.'

They moved forward more cautiously, each busy with his own thoughts and pondering the confrontation to come. Each was glad he was not alone; with the sun beginning to disappear away below them on their left, this seemed now a lonely place to be alone with a murderer.

They saw Robson as they passed beyond the knoll where they had seen his dog. He was finishing an examination of the sheepfold where Wino Willy had kept his vigil with the birds and mammals which seemed to threaten him less than his own kind. Too engrossed in his search to notice them, he moved to the drystone wall which was one of the few impacts man had made on this terrain and began an examination of its crevices. While he worked his way methodically along some eighty yards of wall, they crept to within fifty yards of him without being discerned.

It was Fred who finally gave them away. Spotting his friend Hook, he bounded across the moorland turf with a joyous bark, greeted both men with a tail which threatened to wag his rear end right off, and graciously accepted the fondling of his ears and vigorous patting which was his due.

His master, who seemed to have found what he wanted at the wall, left his search and came across to them. His joviality was almost effusive; Hook would have sworn he was glad to see them.

'And what brings two pillars of the law up here at this time of night? I at least have an excuse for fresh air and exercise.' He indicated Fred, who gyrated his tail in acknowledgement. 'But perhaps you're merely up here to enjoy the sunset on an evening like this.' He looked past them, to where a brilliant crimson segment was all that remained of the sun in the evening sky. Neither of them turned to follow his gaze.

While Fred nuzzled his way insistently into Hook's hand, Lambert walked past Robson to the wall which had been the object of such systematic scrutiny. At this point, the wall ran through a small hollow and was very broad at the base to support its height of some five feet. Lambert removed the large thin stone which Robson had hastily replaced a foot or so from the bottom. From the dry hollow within, he extracted a green anorak and trilby, almost identical with the ones Robson was wearing. Hook's gasp of astonishment made Robson turn to him, so that he was not looking at Lambert when the Superintendent said, 'The wellingtons are no doubt hidden a little further along the wall. Willy wasn't wearing them when you ran him down.'

If Robson thought there was no way out, he gave no sign of it yet. 'You mean the drop-out I used to see up here? Has something happened to him?'

'It was old Fred who let you down,' said Lambert.

By chance, he found the one weakness in his adversary's rock-like calm. Robson whirled instinctively to look at the dog he loved, found no clue to support Lambert's words, and turned back to him for explanation. 'For a start, you were at pains to tell us he was a one-man dog, when he so plainly wasn't. Look at him now.' Fred was sitting with his chin against Hook's knee; each time the Sergeant threatened to desist from fondling his ears, his foot pawed vaguely at the air. The labrador's eyes were almost shut: had he been a cat, he would have been purring.

The Sergeant's thigh was already covered with the fine yellow hairs of the dog's coat. 'There were dog-hairs on the carpet at Lydon Hall,' said Lambert. 'No doubt Fred's, carried there on your clothing. We shall check.' Hook produced an envelope from the inside pocket of his suit and transferred some of the hairs from his trousers into it. 'Fred is almost the

269

opposite of a one-man dog—a most accommodating animal, in fact. If he is happy with me or my sergeant, he would certainly be delighted to take his evening walk with poor, harmless Wino Willy, who had a way with far more timid beasts than Fred.'

'So that makes me a murderer?' said George Robson. It was the first time he had used the word, and it dropped from his lips almost like an admission.

'It was one flaw in your alibi. It made me think of others. For instance, Jane Davidson left a note in Freeman's office altering the time of the Harbens' viewing of Lydon Hall to nine o'clock. He never received it, because he didn't come back into the office, but it was never found. The only other person who could go into Freeman's office without suspicion is you as his deputy.'

Lambert would have had some sympathy with the murderer of Stanley Freeman, though it would have had no effect upon his actions as an instrument of the law. But Robson was now for him the brutal killer of Willy Harrison, and he had to control a surge of hatred. Violence had bred violence, as always. The vandals who slashed trees slashed faces in due course; the louts who began by hitting each other in pub car parks produced the psychopaths who battered old ladies for a few pounds. The murderer who killed because he was cheated by his employer had crushed his innocent

270

accomplice beneath a car a week later, because that very innocence made him dangerous.

'I was up here with Fred when Freeman was killed. You prove otherwise,' said Robson. Now there was desperation in his defiance.

'Oh, I shall. Because you killed Freeman while Wino Willy was up here with Fred. In the clothes you gave him. I expect he thought it was a privilege to walk Fred for you. When we first came across him, Willy had a new pair of boots, and he'd just emptied three bottles of wine. Was that all you paid him for his role as unwitting accessory?' Robson's swift, startled glance showed that he had struck home; Hook wondered if it was the public school training that made a suggestion of meanness strike home when he had brazened out more serious accusations.

Lambert thrust away the image of the summerhouse behind Lydon Hall, with its pathetic trimmings of a ruined spirit, and pressed swiftly on, anxious only now to have this over. 'There were other things, of course, as soon as we thought about it. Both your wife and other dog-walkers confirmed that you have established a pattern of dog-walking over the last two months, slavishly adhering to the same clothes in all weathers and the same hour, between eight and nine. You arranged our first meeting at that time, conveniently forgetting our appointment so that you could draw attention to your dog-walking habits. A strange omission in a man with a reputation for never forgetting appointments. Except of course that it was quite deliberate.'

'Very elaborate!' said George Robson; his short laugh rang loud and brittle in that remote place. 'You have evidence for these flights of imagination, I presume?'

For answer, Lambert spoke no word, but turned and looked back at the wall. In that dry niche which Robson had so recently exposed lay the green anorak and trilby identical to his own, carefully stowed there by the dead hands of Wino Willy.

Robson refused to follow his gaze and said, 'Let me get the detail of this fantastic accusation quite clear for my lawyers.' He was attempting a vein of heavy-handed sarcasm now, but his voice did not hold quite steady enough to reinforce it with the necessary confidence. 'You're saying that I sent Fred up on the common with Willy while I drove my car to Lydon Hall and killed my employer.'

'Not your car,' said Lambert, quietly preparing to remove the last plank from Robson's crumbling story. 'But driven by you. Oh, don't bother arguing!' He found himself shouting in his overwhelming urge to be done with this, to take the callous killer of Willy Harrison away from that innocent's sometime home and put him behind bars. The sound of his own voice surprised him, but it cut

272

Robson's protests dead. The deep-set blue eyes were filled with a horror of the future, the smooth-fleshed face looked suddenly gaunt and old.

'How long had you known about Denise Freeman's affair with Simon Hapgood?' asked Lambert.

There was no fight left in Robson now. He looked at the thin moorland turf by his feet as he said, 'Three months or so. They knew Stanley played away on Wednesdays, so they were safe.'

'And Hapgood always parked in the same place, near the end of the lane to the Freemans' house. If you removed his car and returned it within the hour, you'd be safe enough.'

'How?' said Robson, as if merely curious to test the extent of their knowledge: he had given up denials now.

'You told me yourself the company cars were pool cars, owned by the firm and theoretically available to anyone to drive in an emergency. You keep the keys to all of them in the office.' Robson's shoulders slumped forward; he said nothing.

Lambert said, 'Why try to implicate Hapgood and Denise Freeman?'

'To protect myself.' They noticed the first formal admission, fought down the little spurt of professional satisfaction. 'And they deserved it! Hapgood's an insolent little puppy who

273

thinks he's God's gift to women, and Denise deserves everything she gets if she's going to leap about in bed with a toyboy ten years and more younger than she is!' It was his last flash of animation and bitterness. Lambert remembered the way he had looked at Denise Robson at the funeral. Lust could upset judgement faster than any other emotion.

'No doubt you took Hapgood's car again today to kill poor Willy.' Lambert had to work hard to keep his voice quiet now.

Robson shrugged the bent shoulders hopelessly. 'Willy knew what had happened. Realized it wasn't just the joke I'd suggested when I got him to walk Fred. He wasn't as crazy as I'd thought.'

I could have told you that, thought Lambert, remembering the wild game of quotations he had played with Willy on this very spot. So now a man had to die for being sane: he clenched his fingers quietly within his pockets. In the inverted morality which surrounded the darkest of all crimes, it had its own logic. He nodded now to Bert Hook; he wouldn't trust himself not to let his hatred cloud the formalities.

The Sergeant left the dog and stepped forward with his notebook. 'George Arthur Robson,' he intoned. 'You are charged with the murder of Stanley Freeman. You are not obliged to say anything, but anything you do say will be taken down and may be used in evidence.'

In the twilight at this lonely spot, the familiar formula rang out like the words of a religious ceremony. Lambert thought again of that funeral service, where the suspects had faced each other over the grave through the final rites, and the one genuine mourner had stood unnoticed in the background.

They did not handcuff him, but walked together behind him down the track they had recently climbed so quickly. It took a long time to get back to the car, and Fred's cheerful excursions in search of rabbits and birds made an innocent and inappropriate accompaniment to the journey.

Lambert thought of the woman who waited in vain for Robson at the house to which he would never return. He would tell her himself. He did not know yet that Willy had been, down to her that morning with his deadly tale. Perhaps she would go back to the Dales of her childhood. However affluent her circumstances, she would return to that unforgiving land as a failure after the court case.

By the time they crossed the common in the half-light, the last dog-walkers had departed. Robson sat heavily in the back of the Vauxhall, with Hook beside him and Fred at his feet. Lambert inched the car cautiously forward.

In the last instant before he put on his headlights, he glanced at the dark outline of common and moor above them, where Willy had dwelt for a while with the wild creatures and now would tread no more. The land up there would absorb these deaths as it had thousands of others over the centuries, grinding small the affairs of men, until all was forgotten.